Kincaid and the
Barton Gang

Dan Kincaid was a deputy sheriff in Colorado, but when his teenage sister was brutally murdered by outlaw Matt Barton, he quit his job and went after the killer. His search took him to the Texas Panhandle Diamond B ranch owned by Matt's father, Isaac Barton, who ran the ranch with his second son Ron.

The Diamond B Ranch was a front, and from it, once a year, Matt Barton led a band of men to steal cattle passing along the Western Cattle Trail.

Dan foiled the next operation. The three Bartons were caught and sentenced to hang, but the story had only just begun. Can Dan, now married with a young child, thwart the evil lust for revenge that now threatens him?

Kincaid and the Barton Gang

Alan Irwin

A Black Horse Western

ROBERT HALE · LONDON

© Alan Irwin 2010
First published in Great Britain 2010

ISBN 978-0-7090-8888-2

Robert Hale Limited
Clerkenwell House
Clerkenwell Green
London EC1R 0HT

www.halebooks.com

Typeset by
Derek Doyle & Associates, Shaw Heath
Printed and bound in Great Britain by
CPI Antony Rowe, Chippenham and Eastbourne

ONE PB

Dan Kincaid caught his first sight of his destination in the north of the Texas Panhandle, when he rode out of a gap in a ridge, and saw the town of Larraby ahead of him, to the south. It lay on a flat stretch of ground. Larger than he had expected, it catered for the needs of the surrounding homesteaders and ranches. He rode on into town and stopped at the livery stable. The liveryman, Ben Harper, came out of the stable as he dismounted.

'Howdy,' said Harper, a big man in his thirties, with a cheerful look about him. As he spoke he looked closely at the stranger, a man in his late twenties, tall and broad-shouldered, with a strong, square-jawed face, and fair hair showing underneath his Texas hat.

'Howdy,' said Dan. 'Will you tend to my horse? I aim to stay in town for a spell.'

'Sure,' said Harper. 'You'll find a room at the hotel along the street, and you can get your meals there if you want.'

'I ain't been in these parts before,' said Dan. 'Are there any cattle ranches around here?'

'Only one,' Harper replied, 'and that's the Diamond B Ranch south of here. It's owned by a man called Isaac Barton.'

The liveryman, who had noticed that the stranger was wearing a Colt .45 long-barrelled Peacemaker in a right-hand holster, was curious about the reason for Dan's question. But he refrained from asking.

'Right now,' said Dan, 'I'm just drifting. I've got no particular business here. I aim to rest up for a few days. This looks like a pretty peaceful kind of a town to me.'

'Mostly,' said Harper, 'though the Diamond B hands cause us trouble now and then. But there ain't nothing we can do about that.'

'There's no town marshal, then?' asked Dan.

'No,' replied the liveryman. 'Once or twice we've thought about appointing one, but we couldn't think of anybody who'd be able to stand up to Barton and the kind of men he has on his payroll.'

Dan left his horse at the stable, and walked along to the hotel, where he found the owner, Grant Dixon, in the lobby. Dixon was a small, dapper man, who greeted the stranger with a smile. Dan told him the same story about his presence in town that he had given to the liveryman. He signed the register, took a key from Dixon, and went upstairs to his room, which overlooked the street. It was mid-afternoon.

A little later he left the hotel and walked along to the general store to make a few small purchases. Two horses stood at the hitching rail outside. Dan opened the door and went inside. Two men were standing at the counter. The men were Diamond B hands, Slater and Martin. Both men were over medium height, thickset and unshaven. Each of them was wearing a six-gun. Behind the counter, facing them, was Mary, daughter of the storekeeper Ed Warren, who was out of town for a few days. Mary was a slim, auburn-haired, attractive woman in her mid-twenties. Her face was flushed with anger as she spoke to the two men.

'I want you two men out of here,' she said. 'I don't like the way you're talking to me. I want nothing to do with you. You Diamond B hands seem to think you own this town and everything in it.'

Martin scowled. 'There ain't no need to act so high and mighty,' he said. 'I was figuring that if you came out riding with me one day, we could get better acquainted.'

'I don't want to get better acquainted,' said

Mary, 'and the last thing I'd want to do is go out riding with you. Just leave me be, both of you. I've got a customer to 'tend to.'

Martin's temper flared. He was just about to reply angrily to Mary when Dan spoke. His voice was calm and even, with just a hint of menace. 'You heard the lady,' he said. 'Time for you to leave.'

The two men turned to look at Dan, then stood side by side, facing him.

'You've got a nerve, stranger,' said Martin, his hand and that of his partner moving close to the handles of their six-guns. 'I ain't finished here yet. You're the one who's going to leave. Get moving.'

'Not so,' said Dan. 'The lady don't want you in here, and I don't blame her. She's in charge of this store, and what she says, goes.'

'You'd better think again, stranger,' said Martin. 'You ain't got a chance against the two of us. If you want to stay alive, leave right now.'

Dan remained where he was, nicely balanced, with his right hand close to the handle of his Colt .45.

'Just think it over,' he said. 'I'm pretty good with this Peacemaker. I've got a pretty fast draw, and most of the time I hit exactly what I'm aiming for. So my own guess is that certainly one, and maybe both of you, will go down if you go for your guns. Is it a risk you're willing to take?'

The two men hesitated, eyeing Dan closely.

There was something about him which stifled their impulse to reach for their six-guns. Without another word, they turned and walked out of the store. Watching through the window, Dan saw them mount their horses and ride out of town. Then he turned and walked back to Mary at the counter. She was regarding him with considerable interest. She wondered what had brought this stranger to Larraby.

'I've got to thank you,' she said, 'for getting rid of those two. I never thought I'd see the day when one man would make a couple of Diamond B hands back down like that. But I've got to warn you that if you don't leave town soon, you're going to be in real trouble. Isaac Barton ain't going to like what you just did to two of his men. I'm Mary Warren, by the way. My father owns this store. He's away just now.'

'Dan Kincaid,' said Dan. 'I think I'll stay on a while. This rancher Barton you mentioned. Does he have any family with him?'

'He's a widower,' Mary replied. 'He has one son, Ron, living with him, and another one called Matt I know hardly anything about. I've never seen him. But I did hear that he visits the Diamond B now and then. As for you staying on here, I really did mean it when I said that you might have trouble with Barton. He has a lot of hands on the ranch, some of them meaner than Slater and Martin, the two who've just left here.'

Dan smiled at her. 'Thanks for the warning,' he said, 'but it's a risk I'll just have to take.' He purchased a few small items, then left the store, thinking what an attractive woman it was whom he had just encountered.

Mary walked to the window and watched Dan as he crossed the street on his way to the hotel. She had plenty of admirers in the area, but even on such short acquaintance, the attraction she felt to the stranger was stronger than anything experienced by her before. She felt concerned about the danger he was facing. Then she saw Ben Harper, the liveryman, approaching along the boardwalk, and she walked back to the counter as he came in to the store.

Harper was a close friend of Mary and her father, and she told him of Dan's encounter with the two Diamond B hands.

'Well, I'm darned,' said Harper. 'I wonder how Barton's going to take this? And that goes for his son Ron too. You know what a quick temper he has, and how he fancies himself as a gunfighter.'

'Yes,' said Mary. 'I told the stranger he could be running into trouble, but the notion didn't seem to bother him.'

'He told me he was a drifter,' said the liveryman, 'which gives me an idea. When's your father coming back?'

10

'I'm expecting him back on the noon stage tomorrow,' said Mary.

'Right,' said Harper, 'I'll talk with him as soon as he gets here.'

When Slater and Martin reached the Diamond B, they told Isaac Barton and his son Ron what had happened at the store. The rancher was a man in his fifties, stocky and bearded, with beetling eyebrows and a harsh face. His son, in his early twenties, had been badly spoilt by his father. He was of average height and build, and wore a couple of ivory-handled six-guns. He had an arrogant face, a quick temper, and a firm belief in his prowess as an expert gunfighter. He spoke to the two hands. The contempt in his voice was clear.

'Seems to me,' he said, 'that the two of you should have been able to handle the stranger. My guess is that he was just bluffing. Maybe you two are losing your nerve.'

Martin flushed. 'The way he was acting, I didn't think he was bluffing,' he said, 'and I didn't aim to find out.'

'I'll ride into town in the morning, and cut the stranger down to size,' said Ron Barton.

'Better take Holt with you,' said his father. 'Just in case. He handles a gun better than any of the other hands here.'

'I won't need him,' said Ron, 'but I'll take him if that's what you want.'

After breakfast on the morning of the day after his arrival, Dan left the hotel and walked towards the barber's shop a little way along the street. Reaching it, he went in and sat down in the vacant barber's chair for a shave and a haircut. The barber was still working on him when Ron Barton and Holt rode into town, dismounted at the hotel, and went inside. They came out a little later, and walked towards the barber's shop. As they drew near, Dan came out and started walking along the boardwalk in their direction.

Barton and Holt stopped short as they saw Dan. Sensing the threat to himself from the two men standing side by side facing him, Dan came to a halt as well. As he eyed the two men he guessed that the younger of the two, who was wearing two guns, was Barton's son. He stood ready to explode into action if the need arose.

'You've outstayed your time in Larraby, Kincaid,' said Barton. 'You'll get your horse right now and leave town. You're not wanted here.'

'And if I don't?' asked Dan.

'If you don't, you're a fool,' said Barton. 'You'll end up in the cemetery just outside town.'

'I'm staying,' said Dan. 'I don't take orders from a young upstart who reckons he's handy with a pair of six-guns. I'm—'

He broke off suddenly, and made a draw that was so smooth and speedy that it drew a gasp from the small group of onlookers, including Mary and Harper, who were watching the encounter. Concentrating first on Barton, who was drawing his right-hand gun, Dan shot the gun out of his hand before it had been levelled at its target.

His second shot was aimed at Holt, who was wearing a right-hand gun, and who, confident that Barton was capable of dealing with the stranger on his own, had been slow in reaching for it. The bullet struck Holt in the right arm, and he dropped his revolver. Dan's third shot was directed at Barton, who was recovering from the shock of the first bullet, and was drawing his left-hand gun. But once again he was hit before he levelled the weapon, Dan's bullet hitting him in the left arm. His second gun fell on the boardwalk.

Both men had staggered back a few paces, but were still standing. Keeping them covered, Dan kicked the three guns off the boardwalk, then turned to ask the onlookers whether somebody could get the doctor to come along to the scene of the shooting.

'No need for that,' said a man who, attracted by the shooting, had just arrived on the scene. 'I'm the doctor.'

'Will you take a look at these two, Doc,' asked

Dan, 'and patch them up before I send them back to the Diamond B.'

'All right,' said Doc Bellamy, a short, middle-aged neatly dressed man, whose kindness and efficiency had made him a highly respected figure in the area. 'Bring them along to my place.'

Bellamy led the way, with Holt and Barton walking slowly behind him, clutching their arms. Dan brought up the rear, carrying the three six-guns he had picked up off the street. Inside the doctor's house, Bellamy examined the wounds. Holt's upper right arm had been deeply gouged by a passing bullet. Barton's left arm had suffered the same fate, and his right hand was badly bruised and bleeding. Bellamy cleaned the wounds, and bandaged them. When he had finished, Dan handed the two men their guns, which he had unloaded.

'Time for you two to ride back to the ranch,' he said.

Until then, the two men had been silent, but at long last Barton's anger boiled over.

'This ain't finished, Kincaid,' he said. 'You're going to be sorry you ever came to Larraby.'

'Start moving,' said Dan, curtly. The two men, watched by Dan and the doctor, left the house and walked to their horses, past the group of towns-people out on the street, who were still discussing the shootout. The two wounded men climbed

14

painfully on to their mounts, and headed for the Diamond B.

Back inside the store, Mary and Harper were discussing the gunfight.

'I reckon, Mary,' said the liveryman, 'that we've seen a real top-class shootist in action, and he sure cut Barton down to size. But I'm certain that Kincaid's not a cold-blooded killer. I reckon he could have finished those two off if he'd wanted. I think he put those bullets exactly where he meant to.'

'I reckon you're right,' said Mary. 'What's worrying me now is how Isaac Barton's going to react. He's not going to like his favourite son being treated like this.'

'You're right,' said Harper, 'Kincaid would be wise to leave, but I have a feeling he's set on staying.'

As he finished speaking, they heard the noon stage rolling into town past the store. Harper went to meet the storekeeper as he got off the stagecoach. As they stood on the boardwalk, he told Warren about the two recent encounters between Dan and men from the Diamond B.

'You being leader of the town council, Ed,' he said, 'and me being one of the members, I reckon we should think seriously about offering Kincaid the job of town marshal. It's clear he has grit, and according to him he's just drifting right now. It's time we had some law in this town. It's time Barton and his hands were brought to order.'

'You're right, Ben,' said the storekeeper. 'They went too far when they hassled Mary in the store. But is Kincaid the right man? We know nothing about him. D'you reckon he's a professional gunfighter?'

'If you're asking me whether I think he makes a living hiring out his gun,' said Harper, 'the answer is definitely not. But he sure can handle a six-gun, and we can't afford to be choosy.'

'All right,' said Warren. 'I'll call a meeting of the town council this afternoon, and we'll talk it over.'

The storekeeper called briefly on the hotel owner and the doctor, who were the other members of the town council, to arrange the meeting. Then he went to the store, where Mary gave him her story of the intervention of Dan on her behalf. He told her of the suggestion that Dan be offered the post of town marshal.

'What do you think of Kincaid, Mary?' he asked.

'I like him,' she replied. 'I think he's a good man. I can't understand though, why he's set on staying on here.'

Later that day, when Dan had finished his meal in the hotel dining room, the hotel owner Grant Dixon intercepted him in the lobby. He greeted Dan with a smile, and told him he was a member of the town council, which wished to put a proposition to Dan, and would he meet the council at the storekeeper's house, next to the store, an hour later.

Intrigued, Dan accepted the invitation, and at the appointed time he knocked on the door of the house. Mary answered his knock, and led him to a room where the four council members were congregated. She introduced him to her father, then left the room.

'I'm real grateful to you, Mr Kincaid, for helping Mary out in the store,' said Warren, a tall man in his middle forties, who ran his business efficiently, and was well-liked and respected in the community. 'For a long time the council has felt that we need a town marshal here, to keep order. But we've never been able to find anybody suitable and willing to fill the post. We're hoping you'll take on the job. You know all about the trouble we've had with the Diamond B outfit, and you've shown you can stand up to them. On top of that, we've had strangers passing through now and then who've caused trouble in town. We'll pay you well, and provide a place for you to live, and an office and a jail. What do you say?'

I'll take the job,' said Dan, 'on condition that I can quit at any time, if that's what I want. And in case you're wondering, I'm not in trouble with the law, and I never have been. And that's all I can tell you about myself right now.'

Warren looked at the other three members of the council. They all nodded. He turned to Dan.

'Agreed,' he said. 'When can you start?'

'Right now, if you like,' said Dan.

'All right,' said the storekeeper. 'Stay on in the hotel for a few days. There's an empty house along the street. We'll fix it up as accommodation and an office for you, and build a jail on to the back.'

TWO

When Ron Barton and Holt reached the Diamond B after their encounter with Dan, Isaac Barton was far from pleased. And the following day he was even less pleased when a hand returned from a brief visit to Larraby with the news that Dan had been appointed town marshal. Apart from raising cattle on his ranch, Barton also ran a ruthless cattle-stealing operation during the cattle-drive season. The Western Cattle Trail ran through the Indian Territory, west of the Chisholm Trail, and not far from the border with the northern part of the Texas Panhandle.

The rancher received information from south Texas about the trail herds leaving there along the Western Trail. During each of the past two trail-drive seasons he had select a suitable herd, and had sent men across the border into the Indian Territory to intercept the herd, shadow it, and during the night to kill the trail boss and all the hands. The herd had then been driven over the Kansas border to Dodge City, where it was sold to a buyer, known to Barton, who had no qualms about receiving stolen cattle. By the time the owner of the cattle became aware that they had been stolen, they were on their way by rail to cattle markets in the East. The operations had been highly lucrative, and no suspicion had fallen on Barton and his hands. The rancher spoke to his son, who was with him.

'I ain't happy about having a town marshal in Larraby,' he said. 'I know he's only responsible for upholding the law within the town limits, but the very idea of having a lawman of any sort so close to the ranch makes me nervous. And I don't aim to stand for the way he treated you and the other three men from the ranch.'

'You can leave him to me,' said Ron, still smarting from his encounter with Dan. 'As soon as my right hand has healed up, I'll take a couple of our best hands with me and go after him.'

'No,' said his father. 'First, I'm not sure you're up to it, and second, when he's killed, I don't want suspicion to fall on anybody from the Diamond B. I'm going to call in Raven and Stringer to help us on this. I can get a telegraph message to them in Amarillo, if they're not away on a job. I'll ask them to get here as quick as they can.'

Raven and Stringer were two men who worked together. Their guns were for hire, and no job was too dirty for them if the price was right. They planned their operations meticulously, and so far they had not been suspected of being involved in the murder of any of their victims.

'In the meantime,' the rancher went on, 'tell the hands not to cause any trouble in town. And just keep the lid on that temper of yours if you're anywhere near Kincaid.'

During the week following Dan's arrival in Larraby willing hands converted the empty house to a marshal's office, with sleeping accommodation, and a jail built on at the rear. The jail was accessed from the office. When the work was completed, Dan moved in. He continued to take his meals in the hotel dining room.

Since his encounter with Ron Barton and Holt there had been no further trouble from anyone at the Diamond B. Dan had several conversations with Mary, and the attraction both had felt during their first meeting deepened. She invited him to take supper one evening with herself and her father. Warren, reluctant at first to encourage the friendship between his daughter and a man about whom he knew so little, had eventually agreed to the invitation being given. After the meal, they all sat in the living room. Dan asked Warren what he knew about the Diamond B.

'Not a lot,' answered the storekeeper. 'Barton started raising cattle here about three years ago. Visitors to the ranch ain't encouraged. From the outside it looks like any other cattle ranch, I suppose. But there are some odd things I've noticed. The Diamond B hands are all armed, and mostly have a mean look about them, which is unusual for the ordinary cowhand. And there seem to be a lot more hands than a ranch that size would need. And for the last two years, there's been a time, during the middle of the year, when the amount of food supplies bought from the store for the ranch dropped considerable. It almost looked like a bunch of hands had left the ranch for a while.

'I know that last year Barton sold cows as brood stock to a rancher in Wyoming, but the buyer sent his own hands to drive the cows from the Diamond B to his ranch. And that's about all I can tell you. You know already that he has another son, Matt, who's never been seen in town.'

'I reckon it's about time,' said Dan, 'that I tell you exactly who I am, and why I'm here. But I'm asking you to keep the information to yourselves for the time being. Three years ago I was helping my parents run a ranch in Colorado. My sister Miriam, sixteen years old, was living on the ranch with us. She was a happy girl, full of life, and like me, she was hit pretty hard when our parents both died during a cholera epidemic. Miriam had no interest in ranching, and I figured she'd be happier in town, so we sold the ranch and moved to Saddle Rock, where I got a job as deputy sheriff.

'Things went well for us there, and we soon made friends. One of them was Doc Taylor, who was old enough to be thinking of retiring. Miriam was a special favourite of his, and she often went out with him in his buggy to help him when he was visiting a patient outside town.

'One day, about six months ago, a man robbed the bank in Saddle Rock. I just happened to be nearby when he ran out, and his mask slipped down. He was holding a gun, and he took a shot at me and hit me in the leg before I could fire at him. By the time I was able to fire back he was on his horse and heading out of town. I got two shots in, and his horse seemed to stumble, but picked up again, and he rode on.

'I was losing blood fast from the leg wound, and it was quite a while before I got a posse organized and led it out of town in the direction that the robber had taken. Five miles on, we came across Doc Taylor's buggy, without the horse which had been hitched to it. The robber's horse was standing nearby, head down, with a bad leg wound.'

Dan paused as the painful memories of that dark day in his life came flooding back.

'We found Doc Taylor in the buggy,' he went on, 'with Miriam by his side. They were both dead, shot through the head. And on the floor of the buggy we found the derringer pistol which Taylor used to carry with him when he drove out of town. It hadn't been fired. We did all we could to catch up with the robber, but he vanished without trace.'

'How terrible,' said Mary, sensing Dan's deep feeling of loss. 'Did you know who the robber was?'

'Not until after we'd given up the chase,' Dan replied. 'Then I looked through our file of Wanted posters, and spotted him there. He was Matt Barton, son of the owner of the Diamond B. I quit my job, and set out to find Matt Barton and hand him over to the law. But I just couldn't pick up his trail. Eventually I decided to come to Larraby, in the hope that Matt Barton might show up at his father's ranch one day. That's the reason why I can't say just how long I can stay on here as town marshal. It all depends on whether he turns up, and if so, when. Or whether I get word that he's been seen in some other place.'

'I can see that,' said the storekeeper. 'We're glad to have you in the job just as long as you can stay. But what if Matt Barton comes to the Diamond B for a short spell, and doesn't come into town? How will you know he's there?'

'That *is* a problem,' said Dan. 'I'm counting on him coming into Larraby if he visits the ranch. But

I know we can't be certain about that.'

'I have some ideas that might help,' said Warren. 'Do you have a copy of that poster on Matt Barton?'

'Yes, I do,' said Dan. 'It's in my office.'

'Well,' said Warren. 'I think we should tell the other three members of the council what brought you here. I can guarantee they'll keep it a secret. And if you show them that picture, they can watch out for Matt Barton as well as us. And there's something else I can do. The Diamond B cook comes to the store once or twice a week for supplies. He's a man who likes to hear the sound of his own voice. I'll ask him, casual like, whether Matt Barton ever visits the Diamond B. Maybe he'll let something out that'll help you.'

Dan agreed with the storekeeper's suggestions, and thanked him. Then he went back to his office.

Two days later Dan and Mary left town on horseback for a ride in the surrounding area, and a picnic. When Dan had suggested the ride to Mary, she had agreed without hesitation. When they returned and handed in their mounts at the livery stable the liveryman told them about an incident in the barber's shop not long after they had left town. Two strangers had ridden in from the north, and had gone straight to the barber's shop for shaves and haircuts.

'They were both mean-looking and dirty,' said

Harper, 'like they'd been living rough for a while. The barber finished work on one of them, and had almost done the same on the other, when the man in the chair turned his head suddenly to speak to his partner, and the razor inflicted a cut on the side of his face. He flew into a rage, got out of the chair, and punched Carling, the barber, hard on the face a couple of times, knocking him to the floor. Then the two men left without paying their bills.

'Carling's getting on in years, and he ain't been that well lately,' Harper went on. 'He came in to see me, with the blood streaming down his face, and I took him to Doc Bellamy. He's in there now.'

'Are the two men still in town?' asked Dan.

'In the saloon,' Harper replied.

'Right,' said Dan. 'This is where I start earning my pay. See you both later.'

He checked his Peacemaker, then left them and headed for the saloon. Glancing at Mary, the liveryman saw the look of deep concern on her face as Dan pushed the swing doors open and went inside.

Immediately, Dan saw the two men he was after. They were standing at the bar, with their backs to him. One of them looked over his shoulder as he heard the swing doors open. He saw the badge on Dan's vest, and said something to his partner. They both turned to face Dan, who did not recognize

26

them. Their names were Bell and Yardley. They were robbers who had been operating in Kansas, and had left the state hurriedly, not far ahead of a deputy sheriff. They were heading for South Texas.

Watching the two armed men closely, Dan walked to within a few paces of them, then stopped. He was nicely balanced, and his right hand was close to the handle of his Colt .45.

'I'm arresting you two men,' he said., 'for assaulting the barber and failing to pay his bill. I'm taking you along to the jail. And there'll be a fine to pay as well as the barber's bill.'

Conversation in the saloon had ceased, and customers and the barkeep quickly moved out of the possible line of fire. Dan sensed that the two men were trying to decide whether or not to shoot it out with him and escape. Before they had made up their minds, Dan's Peacemaker suddenly appeared in his right hand, pointing in their direction, and cocked. Impressed by Dan's gun-handling ability, Bell and Yardley slowly raised their hands, and Dan took their guns. Then he escorted them to the jail and locked them in the single cell. Watching from the door of the stable, with Harper by her side, Mary breathed a sigh of relief.

An interested observer of the encounter in the saloon was a Diamond B ranch hand called Carter who, like the other onlookers, had been greatly impressed by the sudden, almost miraculous appearance of the Peacemaker in Dan's right hand. Carter was one of the hands involved in the stealing of the two herds on the Western Cattle Trail. He hurried back to the ranch to tell Isaac Barton and his son Ron about the encounter.

'The more I hear about Kincaid,' said the rancher, 'the more I want to get rid of him. I don't want anything to interfere with our plan for stealing the next suitable trail herd that comes along. I'm hoping Raven and Stringer will be here before long to take care of the marshal.'

THREE

Two days after Dan's encounter with Bell and Yardley in the saloon in Larraby, Raven and Stringer arrived at the Diamond B after nightfall. When they had taken a meal the rancher took them into the living room where his son was waiting. Both men were dressed in black, and had the same bleak look about them. Both were in their forties, slimly built, with a black moustache on the upper lip. The rancher had heard that they were distantly related.

They all sat down, and Isaac Barton gave the two men the full story of Dan's activities since his arrival in Larraby. Raven and his partner were aware that the rancher was involved in criminal activities, though without knowing their exact nature, and they could see why he might wish to eliminate Dan. Then the rancher gave them a further reason.

'I've got big plans for Larraby,' he said, 'and I don't want Kincaid standing in my way. I aim to take over the saloon and the store, and maybe some of the other businesses as well.'

'We'll take the job on,' said Raven. 'But first, we want to know everything you can tell us about Kincaid. We want to know every detail.'

'In that case,' said the rancher, 'I'll get Slater and Martin in here, as well as Holt and Carter. They've all seen Kincaid in action, as well as Ron here.'

When all the men were assembled, Raven and his partner questioned them closely about Dan. Then Raven summed up the situation.

'So we don't know where Kincaid is from, or why he came here,' he said. 'We do know that he don't scare easy, and that when it comes to handling a six-gun he's up among the best. He sleeps in a room next to his office, and he and the storekeeper's daughter have taken a shine to one another. Those two men he put in jail: does anybody know if they're still there?'

'According to the cook who was in town yesterday,' said the rancher, 'they're due to be freed the day after tomorrow. Before they were arrested they had just asked the barkeep how far it was to Amarillo, so it looks like they'll be heading south when they leave town.'

'That's mighty interesting,' said Raven, who already had the germ of an idea in his head. 'One other thing. I expect there are some homesteaders in the area?'

'Sure,' said the rancher, 'mainly to the east of here.'

'Would anybody on the ranch know,' asked Raven, 'whether one of them would be likely to be going into Larraby three days from now?'

'The cook might know,' said the rancher. 'That's one of the days he goes in himself. Go and bring him back here, Holt.'

When the cook came in he told them that each week, on the day in question, a homesteader called Ford drove a buckboard into Larraby, and that he normally left soon after the cook's arrival.

'Right,' said Raven. 'Stringer and me will work out a plan for getting rid of Kincaid without anybody suspecting that the Diamond B had a hand in it. We'll let you know what it is in the morning.'

Two days after the arrival of Raven and his partner at the Diamond B Dan went for breakfast at the hotel. He had been disappointed when the storekeeper told him that he had been unable to get any information from the Diamond B cook about a possible visit by Matt Barton to the ranch. Warren was convinced that the cook just didn't know. After breakfast Dan went back to his office and freed the two prisoners. He had taken, from the money they were carrying, the fine and the barber's and doctor's fees. He handed the rest of the money back to them, but not their weapons. He told them to take a meal and leave town right after.

'And just keep going,' he said. 'I don't want to see you in Larraby again.'

Keeping watch from his office, he saw the two men go into the hotel for a meal, then to the livery stable, where they picked up their horses and paid the liveryman, before riding out of town to the south.

Six miles out of Larraby, Bell and his partner were riding through a narrow, twisting canyon. Rounding a sharp bend, they were suddenly confronted by Raven and Stringer, together with Ron Barton and two ranch hands. Apprehensive, and unarmed, they stopped abruptly at the sight of the six-guns trained on them.

'I know that Marshal Kincaid has been holding you two men in Larraby,' said Raven, 'so I reckon you ain't exactly the best of friends. I guess he told you to leave the area pronto, and never ride into Larraby again.'

'That's right,' said Bell, wondering what this was leading up to.

'Well,' said Raven, 'it so happens we don't like him either, and we aim to get rid of him once and for all. You can help us with this, without any danger to yourselves. And when you've done what we want you can ride on south with an extra two hundred dollars apiece, paid in advance. Are you interested?'

Bell had a feeling that a refusal to help could prove costly for him and his partner. 'Sounds good to me,' he said, looking at Yardley, who nodded. 'What do we have to do?'

Raven explained to the two men his plan for dealing with Dan, which was to be put into operation the following day. Then they all rode to the Diamond B.

The following day homesteader Ford made his usual journey into Larraby. From his homestead he normally headed north-west until he reached the southern end of the canyon in which Bell and his partner had been stopped the previous day. Then he would ride through the canyon and on to Larraby. On this particular day, about an hour before noon, he was halfway between his homestead and the canyon when he saw a couple of men who appeared to be camping just off the trail. There were bedrolls lying on the ground, and a campfire was burning.

As Ford passed close by he was surprised to see that the two men were Bell and Yardley. On the day they were arrested in Larraby he had been on a special visit to see the doctor, and he had seen Dan taking the two men to jail. They were standing, and looking towards him as he passed them. They appeared to be unarmed, and made no attempt to stop him as he continued on his way.

When he reached town he left the buckboard outside the store and went to see Dan in his office. He told him about seeing Bell and his partner.

'It looked like they were settling down there for a spell,' said Ford. 'I figured you'd like to know.'

'I'm obliged,' said Dan. 'I don't want them hanging around. I told them to leave town and keep on riding south. Tell me exactly where they are, and I'll ride out there right now. Did you see if they had any weapons?'

'Not as far as I could tell,' said Ford.

Dan took off his badge and put it in his upper vest pocket. Then he went to the store to tell Warren where he was going. He left town, riding south. Passing through the canyon where Bell and his partner had been stopped the previous day, he rounded the same bend where this had occurred, and was suddenly confronted by Raven and Stringer, on foot, with their six-guns trained on him. To resist would have been suicidal. His Peacemaker was taken from him and he was ordered to dismount. Then he was bound hand and foot, blindfolded, and slung over the back of his horse.

Leading Dan's horse, Raven and his partner went for their own mounts, then rode out of the canyon, and to the place where Ford had seen Bell and his partner. They were still there. They stood watching as Dan was pulled off his horse and was laid on his back on the ground. As a professional assassin, Raven knew exactly how to direct a bullet into the heart. Standing over Dan, he took careful aim at the marshal's chest with his six-gun, and fired one shot. Dan's body jerked, then he lay motionless.

Raven holstered his gun, then he and Stringer walked up to Bell and Yardley.

'Like you see,' said Raven, 'the plan worked. You two can be on your way, with the money we gave you.'

'All right,' said Bell. 'Did you bring those six-guns you promised us?'

You can take the ones we're wearing,' said Raven. He and Stringer pulled out their guns, raised them, and each of them sent a bullet into the heart of the man standing in front of him. Bell and his partner were killed instantly.

Quickly, Raven and Stringer untied the ropes binding Dan's hands and feet, and removed the blindfold. They fired two shots into the air from his six-gun, and laid the weapon on the ground nearby. Then they took two extra fully loaded six-guns which they had brought with them and fired each gun, once, into the air. They dropped one gun on the ground near Bell, the other near his partner. Last of all they took from Bell and Yardley the $400 they had been paid, and rode off quickly towards the Diamond B.

When Raven had fired at Dan, the marshal lost consciousness for a while, but came to just after the ropes and blindfold had been removed. He stayed motionless and watched Raven and Stringer through half-closed eyes as they finished setting the scene intended to pin the death of himself on to Bell and Yardley. When Raven and his partner rode off, Dan waited till they were out of sight. Then he tried to get up. He rose to his knees, then collapsed and lay motionless on the ground.

This was how Ford found him when, forty minutes later, he drove up on his way back to the homestead. He stopped close to the three bodies lying on the ground, jumped down, and ran over to look at them, one by one. He was sure that Bell and Yardley were dead, but Dan, though unconscious, was still breathing. A big, strong man, he managed to lift Dan on to the floor of the buckboard, on top of the two bedrolls which he found lying near the fire. He turned the buckboard and drove it back to Larraby as quickly as he could, bearing the welfare of his passenger in mind. Upon reaching his destination he stopped outside the doctor's house, and he and the liveryman, who had seen him arrive, carried the still unconscious man inside, and laid him on a table.

Leaving the doctor to tend to the wounded man, Ford and Harper went to the store, where they told Warren and his daughter how Dan had been found wounded, and was now with Bellamy.

Doc Bellamy could see the bullet hole in Dan's vest. As he removed the garment he felt something in the pocket, underneath the hole. He put his fingers inside the pocket and pulled out the marshal's badge. It was made of soft metal, and a hole had been drilled almost through its centre. He laid the badge on the table, just as Mary knocked on the door. He let her in.

'I've just heard that Dan's here,' she said. 'Maybe I can help?'

The doctor beckoned to her to follow him as he went back to his patient. Deeply concerned, Mary watched as Bellamy examined the wound, which had been bleeding. He probed inside it, and could feel the bullet, not far below the surface of the skin. Carefully, he extracted it, and treated the wound. Looking at the badge, he was sure that it had slowed down the bullet, and had undoubtedly saved Dan's life. He showed it to Mary.

'He owes his life to this, I reckon,' he said. 'I think he'll pull through all right, but it's going to take a while. I'm hoping he'll come round soon.'

Relieved, Mary sat close to Dan. Five minutes later she saw his eyes open and he looked at her. She called the doctor, and a moment later he came into the room and stood by her side.

'Where am I?' asked Dan, weakly.

'You're in Larraby,' said Bellamy. 'Ford found you and brought you back here. I just took a bullet out of you. I reckon you're going to be all right.'

Dan asked Mary if she would go and bring her father back to see him. He asked her not to give anybody the idea that he was out of danger.

Warren closed the store and went to the doctor's house with Mary. They stood with the doctor close to Dan. He looked up at them.

Haltingly, he told them how he had been captured by two strangers in the canyon, taken to the place where he was found, and shot.

'I didn't see who shot me,' he said, 'but when I came to a bit later on, saw Bell and Yardley lying on the ground. Then I saw the two men who had captured me fire a few bullets into the air before they rode off.'

'What did those two men look like?' asked Warren.

Dan told them, but Warren and the others failed to recognize the descriptions.

'It's clear,' said Dan, 'that it was all a plan to kill me, and put the blame on Yardley and Bell. But who set it up? Who are the two strangers? I have a strong feeling that Isaac Barton is behind it. And maybe he hired those two men to do the job.'

He paused for a moment to collect his thoughts, then continued:

'I have a plan,' he said, 'but it needs to be approved by the town council. I'd like everybody outside the council to be told I've died from the bullet wound. I'd like a coffin to be buried that's supposed to have me inside. If this isn't done, and Barton knows I'm still alive and wounded, then maybe somebody else, besides myself, is going to get hurt by his men or those two killers he's hired. But if he thinks I died without saying anything, then as soon as I'm fit I can stay under cover and make some night-time visits to the Diamond B to see if I can find out exactly what is gong on there.'

'What you say makes sense,' said Bellamy. 'You can stay here in hiding with me.'

'Mary,' said Warren. 'Go and bring Grant Dixon and Ben Harper here. Tell them it's urgent council business.'

When Mary returned with the two men, Warren told them of Dan's proposal, and after some discussion it was agreed. The undertaker would have to be told of the deception, but he was a man who could be trusted to keep a secret.

Warren went to see the undertaker, and later that day the word was passed around town that Dan had been killed by Bell and Yardley, whose bodies were being brought back to town for burial. The following morning, the weighted coffin, supposedly containing Dan's body, was buried in the town cemetery. The ceremony was watched by ranch hand Slater of the Diamond B, who was in town at the time. He returned to the ranch with the news, and later in the day Raven and Stringer left for Amarillo, carrying the handsome payment that Barton had handed them for their services. In Larraby, hidden in the doctor's house, with Mary calling after dark each day to sit with him for a while, Dan continued to make a steady recovery.

FOUR

Two and a half weeks after Dan had been wounded by Raven, Doc Bellamy told him that he was fit enough to start on whatever it was he was aiming to do. During Dan's recovery hands from the Diamond B had visited town from time to time, but they had caused no trouble. During the evening, Warren came to see Dan at the doctor's house. Bellamy was present.

'For the time being,' said Dan, 'I don't aim to draw any marshal's pay, since I'm not doing the job. But I've got to find out why Barton was so set on getting rid of me. And you know that I want to catch up with his son Matt. So I'm going to pay some visits to the ranch, after dark. Maybe I'll hide out somewhere near the ranch during the daytime. It's the only way I can think of to find out what's going on there. It would help if I knew something about the layout of the ranch buildings.'

'I can help you there,' said Bellamy. 'I've been there a couple of times.' He went on to give the information that Dan wanted. Then the storekeeper spoke.

'That's a real dangerous mission you're going on,' he said. 'If you're caught, Barton'll make sure you're dead this time.'

'I know you're right,' said Dan, 'but I'm hoping to catch them off guard. They've got no reason to think somebody might be nosing around. I'll leave town after dark tomorrow. I'll take provisions with me, and it could be I won't be back here for a week or more.'

Just after nightfall the following day Mary went along to see Dan at the doctor's house.

'Came to wish you luck,' she said. 'I know what you're aiming to do. And I know it's dangerous. But we're hoping we'll see you back here before long.'

'If I can get proof,' said Dan, 'that Isaac Barton is involved in any sort of crime, I aim to come back here and call in the law.'

Mary left, and immediately after, Dan went to the stable, making sure he was unobserved. Ben Harper had his horse ready for him, with a sack of provisions and a bedroll. Avoiding the main street, Dan rode quietly out of town, and headed for the Diamond B. As he closed the stable door, the liveryman wondered whether he would ever see

Dan again. Then he glanced at the stall just vacated by Dan's horse. He hoped that its absence would not be noticed. He would have to think up some plausible explanation in case he was asked about it.

Dan rode as quickly as possible towards the Diamond B. When he saw the lights from several of the buildings ahead of him he looked around for a place to leave his horse. He found a deep gully, well off the trail, about 400 yards from the buildings. He secured his horse, and walked towards the lights, then circled the buildings at a distance. As far as he could tell there were no guards stationed outside the buildings. Then, just as he was about to move closer, a door opened, and in the light which streamed out he saw a number of men leave the building and go into another one close by. He guessed that he had just seen the hands, having finished supper, leaving the cookshack for the bunkhouse. He had a sudden thought. If he could eavesdrop on the conversation of these men, maybe he would pick up some of the information he was after.

He waited for a short while, to make sure all the hands had left the cookshack, then he moved round, and approached the bunkhouse from the rear. His luck was in. The night was warm, and there was a wide-open window in the rear wall of the bunkhouse which would not be in view of anyone walking between the buildings. As he approached the open window, he could hear the sound of voices inside the building. He stood by the side of the window, his back pressed against the wall, straining to hear what was being said.

He remained in that position until the lamps were turned off inside and all talk ceased. Some parts of the conversation he had not heard properly, but from the rest he had gleaned some very useful information. It appeared that on the following morning some of the hands were riding east to the Western Cattle Trail to pick up a trail herd belonging to the Lazy Y Ranch in South Texas, and take it on to Dodge City. What was meant by 'pick up' was not clear. It could have meant 'steal'. It could have meant 'take over legitimately'. But of great interest to Dan was the information that Matt Barton was to join the men at some point after they had left the ranch, and was to take charge of the operation.

Dan had not heard his own name mentioned, but there had been talk of two men called Raven and Stringer, who had been paid off by Isaac Barton, and had left for Amarillo. The names meant nothing to Dan, but he thought it possible that they could be the men who had captured him in the canyon.

Dan returned to his horse in the gully. He had decided that in the morning he would follow the

Diamond B hands when they left the ranch in the direction of the Western Cattle Trail. He took his bedroll down from his horse, and snatched a few hours' sleep before dawn.

It was two hours after daybreak when he saw a group of ten riders leave the ranch buildings, heading a little north of east. He waited a while, then left the gully from the end not visible from the ranch buildings, and followed the riders at a distance, taking care that they did not become aware of his presence. His pursuit continued without incident, and just before nightfall he saw the riders stop and set up camp for the night. He guessed that they were not far from the border with the Indian Territory.

He waited where he was until darkness had set in, then he rode towards the camp. He stopped 200 yards short of the campfire, and secured his horse in the middle of a small group of trees off the trail. He continued on foot towards the campfire, halted for a moment, then circled it once. He could see that it was located close to the sheer wall, about ten feet high, of a low rock outcrop which stood alone on a flat stretch of ground. The side of the outcrop remote from the campfire was not steep, and it looked climbable. The ten men had just finished a meal, and were all seated on the ground near the fire.

Dan circled around, and approached the

sloping side of the outcrop. He climbed it without difficulty. When he reached the flat top he lay down and wormed his way along it until his head was close to the top of the sheer wall, the foot of which was only a short distance from the fire. He dared not raise his head to look at the men below, for fear of being seen, but he could hear their voices quite clearly. And once again, the spell of eavesdropping was to bring him some very useful information.

But before that happened, and just as he was settling down to listen to the conversation, he heard somebody hailing the camp from the surrounding darkness. Shortly after this he heard the men below greeting the one who had just arrived in camp. From these greetings it was clear that the name of the newcomer was Matt. At last, thought Dan, he had made contact with the outlaw for whom he had been searching so long.

After taking some food and drink Matt Barton discussed the forthcoming operation in detail with the others. Listening from above, Dan gathered that in the morning they intended to ride to a point overlooking the Western Cattle Trail, where they would await the arrival of the Lazy Y herd from the south. They would shadow the herd, and would take it over by force at the first night stop made by the herd after crossing the border into Kansas. Then they would drive it on to Dodge City, where a buyer was waiting.

Barton told the others that he expected one of his own men, Tyler, to ride into camp that evening. Tyler had signed on as a trail hand at the beginning of the trail drive, with orders to quit the drive at the appropriate time, so as to meet up with Barton and the others at the outcrop on this particular day, in order to give them the exact location of the Lazy Y herd. Tyler was able to tell them that the herd would now be bedded down at a point just about due east of the outcrop. And it would almost certainly be driven over the border into Kansas in three days' time. Although there were bound to be other trail herds on the Western Cattle Trail at that time of year, he did not think that the Lazy Y trail herd was being closely followed by, or was close behind, any other herd. Barton then said that they would steal the herd after midnight on the day that it was driven over the border.

It was now almost midnight. The men around the campfire took to their bedrolls, and soon all was quiet below Dan. He twisted round, crawled along for a few yards, then rose to his feet, and crouching down, made for the top of the sloping side of the outcrop. But he was only halfway there, moving along the edge of the flat top, where there was a slight overhang, when suddenly the ground gave way under his feet. Only a supreme effort on his part prevented him from falling over the edge.

The horses were picketed directly below Dan, and the material he had dislodged fell down onto the heads of several of them. They squealed in terror, broke away from the picket line, and ran off. Dan hurried down the slope to the ground below, and ran towards the place where he had left his horse. As he was drawing near to it he saw two of the horses which had run off from the camp. They were standing still. He went on to his horse, and was just about to mount it and ride off, when he heard the sound of approaching voices. Looking out from inside the cluster of trees, he saw that one of the horses had followed him, and was standing about five yards from the nearest tree. He heard two men speaking to one another, then saw the dim shape of one man as he approached the horse standing nearby. The man stopped near to it, speaking quietly to calm it down.

Dan stayed motionless, praying that his own mount would make no sound or movement to attract the attention of the man he was watching. Then he saw that the horse was being led off towards the camp, and soon it disappeared into the darkness. He waited a while until all was quiet again, then he left the shelter of the trees, circled round the camp, and rode off to the east. He continued steadily in that direction with one break, during which he took some food and drink. Crossing the border into the Indian Territory, and still heading east, he arrived at daybreak at the Western Cattle Trail, where a wide stretch of ground had been trampled flat by the hoofs of countless cattle moving north.

Dan walked across the trail, examining it closely. He was sure that a herd had been driven along it sometime during the past twenty-four hours. He mounted his horse, and rode north along the trail. Half an hour later he came in sight of the Lazy Y trail herd and the camp close by, with the chuck wagon and remuda. The trail boss, Snyder, and the hands, who had just finished breakfast, looked curiously at Dan as he rode up to them and stopped.

'Howdy,' said Dan. 'I'd like a few words with the trail boss.'

'That's me,' said Snyder, a tall lean man in his early fifties, with a good reputation as a trail boss in previous years.

'Could I have a word in private?' asked Dan.

'All right,' said Snyder. Dan dismounted and walked with him out of earshot of the trail hands. 'Who are you, and what's this all about?'

Quickly, Dan told the trail boss about Matt Barton's intention, with the help of a gang of eleven men, to steal the herd during its first night in Kansas. He explained how he happened to be involved.

49

'This is quite a story,' said Snyder, 'and pretty hard to believe. I can't see why you would make it up. But have you got any proof?'

'Maybe I have,' Dan replied. 'Are you missing a trail hand called Tyler?'

Snyder's eyebrows lifted. 'I am,' he said. 'He was riding drag yesterday morning, and he slipped off without anybody noticing. I couldn't figure why.'

'When I was eavesdropping on Matt Barton and the others last night,' said Dan, 'Tyler rode into the camp, and told Barton exactly where your herd was located, and when you would be crossing the border into Kansas. It seemed he was working for Barton. D'you think any more of your hands might be doing the same?'

'Damn!' said the trail boss. 'I thought Tyler was a bit on the shifty side. I'd never met him before, and I only took him on because one of the hands who was due to go with me took sick. The rest of the crew with me, all six of them, I know pretty well. There's no chance they would be in cahoots with Barton.'

'Good,' said Dan. 'The question now is, how do we get the better of Barton. Even with me helping out, we're badly outnumbered. And Barton and his men are all killers, and used to handling guns.'

'We all bring a gun with us on a trail drive,' said Snyder, 'and we'd all put up a fight if the herd was in danger of being stolen. But we're more used to handling cows than guns. You got any notion how we should deal with this?'

'I have,' said Dan. 'I reckon you should carry on with the drive as if you had no idea you were being shadowed by Barton and the others. And I'll ride on ahead of you.'

Dan went on to give the details of his plan, and Snyder agreed with him that it looked like the best solution to the problem.

'You'll need to make good time,' he said, 'but before you leave, I'll get the cook to rustle up some breakfast for you.'

Half an hour later, Dan was in the saddle, riding at a fast pace towards the north.

FIVE

Riding along the Western Cattle Trail, Dan crossed the border into Kansas during the evening of the day on which he had left the Lazy Y herd. He camped near the border, and rode on to Dodge City the following day. He arrived there in the afternoon, and went to the sheriff's office. He was hoping to find a deputy sheriff there called Jim Fleming, with whom he had become friends when they were both lawmen in Colorado. Fleming had transferred to Dodge not long before Dan quit his job.

His luck was in. Inside the office he found both his old friend Jim, and Sheriff Dawson, a lawman nearing the end of his career, with a reputation as an honest and fearless peace officer. Surprised, Jim walked up to Dan as he entered the office.

'Dan!' he said. 'I'm sure glad to see you. I heard about Miriam. Tried to get in touch with you at

Saddle Rock, but you'd left. I heard you were after Matt Barton.'

'That's right,' said Dan. 'I need some help. Figured to have a talk with Sheriff Dawson.'

Jim introduced Dan to the sheriff, who was sitting at his desk. Dan told him about the murder of his sister, and subsequent events which had led him to Dodge City.

'I'm pretty certain,' he said, in conclusion, 'that the Lazy Y herd will cross the border into Kansas tomorrow, and that tomorrow night Barton and his gang are planning to steal the herd after midnight. I was hoping that maybe a posse could ride back along the Western Cattle Trail with me tomorrow, and join the Lazy Y trail crew soon after dark. That way, we would be able to surprise the raiders and capture them without too much blood being shed.'

Dawson, who had been listening closely to Dan, leaned back in his chair.

'All this is mighty interesting,' he said. 'Trail herds were stolen in the same area last year and the year before, and the trail crews were killed. We never got close to finding out who the robbers were, but it could have been the same gang as the one you're talking about. This is a great chance to get our hands on them. We'll get a posse of a dozen men together tomorrow morning, and Jim here will lead them.'

'Right,' said Dan. 'I'll be ready to leave with the posse. There is one other thing. Listening to Barton and his men, I overheard some talk about a crooked cattle-buyer who was waiting here in Dodge City to take over the herd from Barton, knowing it was stolen. His name is Gorman. D'you know him?'

'I do,' said the sheriff, 'and if I remember right, he was in town last year and the year before. With the herd moving ten or twelve miles a day, I guess he'll be expecting it to turn up here in four or five days from now. I aim to arrest him today, and throw him in a cell before he gets wind of the posse going after the gang and leaves town. Then we'll put him on trial later, with the others.'

The posse departed a little before noon the following day. It halted about fourteen miles north of the border. Jim Fleming sent a rider with experience as an army scout to check on the position of the trail herd, and to find out whether it was being shadowed. He returned shortly after nightfall, to say that the day's drive had been completed, and the herd was being held about six miles south. He also reported that he had seen, through field glasses, a camp about four miles south of the herd's present position, a little way off the trail. In the camp he had seen a number of men moving around, but couldn't get close enough to say exactly how many. They had a

54

campfire going, so it looked like they were staying there for a while.

The posse rode on south, until they came in view of the Lazy Y campfire, with the herd bedded down nearby. Dan rode on ahead and, as soon as he was recognized by the trail boss, he called on Jim and the others to ride into camp. Greatly relieved to see them, Snyder said that they had seen no sign of the outlaws who were shadowing them.

'They're waiting about four miles south of here,' said Dan, 'likely aiming to ride in after midnight, like they said. This gives us a little time to work out a plan to deal with them when they get here.'

The trail boss, with Dan and the leader of the posse, walked round the camp, and then to the bedded herd, which Snyder's crew had driven into a circular, shallow depression in the ground, just large enough to accommodate the herd. There was a small grove of trees at one point on the edge of the depression. The two night guards were circling the herd on their horses in opposite directions. Quietly, the trail boss called out to each of them as they passed him, to let them know that the posse had arrived. Then he spoke to Dan and Jim.

'There's a small box canyon close by,' he said. 'I thought of driving the herd in there, but it's on the small side, and I figured this was better.'

'That canyon sounds interesting,' said Dan. 'I reckon we should take a look at it when we leave here.'

They rode round the depression, spending some time inside the grove of trees. Then they rode on to take a good look at the canyon nearby. The entrance was about twelve feet wide, the walls on each side were sheer, and the floor was fairly flat. The three men discussed the situation, and came to a decision that the camp should be moved immediately from its present position into the canyon. They rode back to the camp, and half an hour later, still with plenty of time to go before midnight, the chuck wagon, campfire, remuda and trail crew, except for the two night guards, were in the canyon with the posse.

Two members of the posse were sent out to watch for the arrival of the Barton gang, in case they had decided to strike earlier than originally planned. Inside the canyon, five bedrolls were taken from the chuck wagon, and each one was stuffed with brush to give the appearance of containing a sleeping man. They were then laid on the ground not far from the campfire.

The trail boss rode off to tell the two night guards of the plan for dealing with the expected attack, then he returned to the canyon. The cook prepared a meal for the posse. Then they all settled down to wait.

*

The two men who had been sent out to watch for the approach of Barton and his men left their horses a little way to the east of the gang's camp, and advanced on foot in the darkness. They got close enough to see that there were twelve men there, taking a meal. After they had finished this, they sat talking, but they were too far away for the two men watching to hear what they were saying. At half an hour after midnight they all rose together, and the fire was doused. The two watching men ran to their horses and rode as fast as they could to the Lazy Y camp. Riding into the canyon, they gave the news that the gang of twelve men was not far behind them.

The men inside the canyon quickly ran out, leaving the fire burning brightly, and the bedrolls lying on the ground. Dan, with two other men from the posse, ran to the grove of trees close to the bedded herd. The rest hurried to hide at various points around the top of the canyon wall.

The gang, led by Matt Barton, stopped well short of the herd, and one man was sent ahead to find the exact locations of the camp and the cattle. He cane back with the news that the herd was bedded down, with two night guards, and that the rest of the trail crew were sleeping in a box canyon close by.

57

Barton sent three men to dispose of the night guards, with strict orders to kill the two men, and to do the job without stampeding the cattle. Two of the men carried a knife, and each was proficient in its use as a killing weapon, either by throwing, or by driving it in at close quarters.

One of the men went ahead on foot and circled the herd, skirting the grove, and noting that the guards were passing one another at two points well away from the trees. He returned to the others, and the plan decided on was that the two men with knives would hide in the trees with the third. They would step out behind each guard as he passed, and throw two knives into his back. The third man would drag the guard from his horse, and pistol-whip him to keep him quiet, if this was necessary.

The three men approached the side of the grove remote from the herd, and secured their horses. Hidden among the trees, Dan and his two companions, Arnold and Emery, saw the three figures outlined against the night sky as, side by side, they entered the grove, with a short space between them, and started moving towards the other side. Hidden behind tree trunks, Dan and his companions each selected a separate intruder for his attention. Two of the men were pistol-whipped on the head by Dan and Emery as they passed. The third was put out of action by Arnold, a big powerful man, who grabbed his victim by the neck from behind, and maintained a stranglehold until the man, like his two partners, was unconscious. The three prisoners were quickly bound and gagged, and the night guards were told what had happened.

Outside the canyon entrance Barton and the others waited a while to give the three men time to deal with the night guards watching the herd. Then they cautiously moved up to the entrance on foot, and paused to look into the canyon. The campfire was burning brightly, and they could see, dimly, the outlines of the five stuffed bedrolls lying on the ground. With Barton leading, the men ran silently up to the bedrolls, and fired several bullets into each one.

The sound of gunfire inside the canyon alerted the trail crew and lawmen outside, and four riflemen moved quickly to points above the canyon entrance. The rest stayed at their positions at various points on the rim.

The men inside the canyon soon realized that they had been firing at dummies, and made for the exit from the canyon. But they were met by a hail of bullets which killed two of them before the rest withdrew in confusion, uncertain as to what their next move should be. Then they heard Jim Fleming shouting down from above.

'We know you're down there, Barton,' he said. 'There's a posse of lawmen up here, as well as the trail crew. You're outnumbered. We've got men all round the rim. Anybody else trying to leave the canyon will be shot dead. And we're taking care of the men you sent to kill the night guards. Come daylight, you'll come out unarmed, one by one.'

Barton, realizing that any attempts at resistance would be futile, wondered how it had come about that their plan to steal the herd had become known to the law. At dawn he was the first one to throw down his weapons and leave the canyon, to join the three men whom he had sent to kill the night guards. The rest followed him, one by one.

'This is a great haul,' said Jim to Dan, who had joined him soon after the shooting stopped. 'And all done without a single casualty on our side. We'll bury the two dead men here and take the others to Dodge on their horses. That's where they'll be tried. You'll be needed there to give evidence.'

'Sure,' said Dan. 'I'll go along with you.'

Two hours later they departed with the prisoners. The grateful trail boss and crew, ready to put the herd on the trail again, knew that but for Dan they would now most likely be dead. When the posse reached Dodge, and stopped outside the sheriff's office, Dawson came out and inspected the prisoners with grim satisfaction. A group of interested spectators gathered. The prisoners were escorted to their cells, and Dan and Jim went into the office with the sheriff, where they gave him the details of the successful operation.

'That's real good news,' said Dawson. 'I have the buyer Gorman in jail. We'll put him up for trial with the others.'

'I reckon,' said Dan, 'that we should let the US marshal in Amarillo know that Isaac Barton on the Diamond B in the Texas Panhandle has been organizing the theft of trail herds, and that we've caught his son Matt and his men red-handed. The marshal needs to have Isaac Barton and his men on the ranch picked up before word gets to Barton that his son and the men with him are either dead or in jail.'

'You're right,' said Dawson. 'I'm going to get a message off right away.'

Dan left the others and went to the telegraph office to send a message to the storekeeper and his daughter in Larraby. In case the telegraph operator there was in cahoots with Isaac Barton, Dan had agreed a code with Warren before he left. He would sign any telegraph message sent by him with the name 'Sullivan', and in the message he would let the storekeeper know when he was likely to turn up again in Larraby. He sent the following message, addressed to the storekeeper: EXPECT TO CALL ON YOU IN LARRABY SEVEN OR EIGHT DAYS FROM NOW REGARDING NEXT ORDER OF CLOTHING. LAST BUSINESS VENTURE WENT VERY WELL INDEED AND HAS BEEN COMPLETED SATISFACTORILY. SULLIVAN.

While awaiting trial, and in the hope that it would reduce his sentence, Gorman, the cattle buyer, confessed to the sheriff that in each of the past two years he had taken over from Matt Barton a trail herd, knowing it to be stolen. And having been given the chance of seeing the men who had been brought in with Barton, and were now in the cells, he confirmed that these men were the same as those who had killed the trail crews and had brought the two stolen trail herds into Dodge last year and the year before.

Three days later, when the trial took place, Gorman repeated the information given to the sheriff, and Dan's testimony was also heard. As Matt Barton listened to this, he realized that this one man was the cause of his downfall, and that likely his father and the men at the Diamond B would by now have been arrested. Staring at Dan with a murderous glare, he vowed that in the unlikely event of his escaping before any sentence was carried out, his first mission would be to hunt down and kill Dan.

The verdict in respect of Matt Barton and his men was guilty of murder and robbery. They were all sentenced to be hanged. Gorman was found guilty of receiving stolen cattle, and was given a long prison sentence.

After the trial, Dan went to see the sheriff in his office. Dawson told him that, as he had expected, the hangings would take place in two or three days' time.

'No need for me to wait till then,' said Dan. 'I reckon I'll leave for Larraby in the morning, and find out if the law has picked up Isaac Barton and his men yet.'

SIX

Dan timed his arrival in Larraby to take place after dark. He rode up behind the store without being seen, secured his horse there, and knocked on the door to the living quarters. It was opened by Mary.

She gave him a big smile. 'Welcome back,' she said. 'We got your message. We've been expecting you. Come and see Father.'

She led him into the living room, where her father was seated. Dan and Mary sat down.

'We sure are glad to see you back here alive,' said Warren. 'We've had our own share of excitement here. Five nights ago, a posse of Texas Rangers from Amarillo raided the Diamond B while everyone there was in bed, and they took Isaac Barton and all his men prisoner. They're going on trial in Amarillo. One of the rangers told us about you joining up with a posse from Dodge to capture Matt Barton and his men. We're real

64

interested to hear how you managed to get the better of those cattle thieves.'

Dan gave the details of what happened since he left Larraby. He told them that, from what he had heard while eavesdropping on the gang, Matt Barton normally worked alone, but his father had persuaded him to take charge, once a year, of a cattle-stealing operation on the Western Cattle Trail.

Mary insisted on preparing a meal for Dan, and after he had taken this, he sat down again with her and her father.

'What are your plans now?' asked the storekeeper. 'The marshal's job is still yours if you want it. I know there'll be no more trouble from Isaac Barton's men, but we get our share of tough-looking characters calling here. Most folks in town feel happier with a lawman around.'

'I appreciate the offer,' said Dan, 'and it's something I'll think on. But first, I reckon I'll be needed at Amarillo for the trial.'

'I know,' said Warren, 'that the telegraph operator is holding a message from Amarillo for you. Maybe that's about the trial.'

'I'll pick it up in the morning when the office opens,' said Dan, 'and let you know what it's about. Meanwhile I'll get me a room at the hotel.'

Mary accompanied Dan to the door. She stepped outside with him, and closed it behind her.

'When you left here,' she said, 'I was pretty scared about what might happen to you. But it looks like everything has turned out all right.'

'Now that the law has Matt Barton,' said Dan, 'I can get on with my life. Which means I can ask you something I wanted to the very first time we met. I reckon we belong together, and I'm hoping you feel the same way. To come right out with it, I reckon it's time we saw a preacher. How does the idea strike you?'

She smiled at him. 'I'm taking that as a proposal of marriage,' she said, 'and I'm all in favour of the idea. You're a good man, Dan Kincaid, and the only man I ever took a real fancy to. I reckon we're right for one another. I think we should get married right after the trial is over.'

'I was hoping you'd say that,' said Dan, 'but how's your father going to take it?'

'He ain't blind,' said Mary. 'He knows how I feel about you. He'll be glad for me. What we have to start thinking about is what we do and where we settle down after the wedding.'

Dan kissed her. 'Let's talk about it tomorrow,' he said, 'after I've been to the telegraph office.'

Dan handed his horse in at the livery stable and took a room at the hotel. The liveryman and hotel keeper, both pleased to see him back, listened as he gave a brief account to each of them of the capture of Matt Barton and his men.

The following morning, Dan went to the telegraph office to pick up the message. It was from the US marshal in Amarillo. It was a request that Dan travel on to Amarillo as soon as possible, to give evidence at the trial. Dan took the message to the store and showed it to Mary and her father.

'I'd best leave for Amarillo right now,' he said. 'I'll get back as soon as I can.'

Mary accompanied him to the door, and it was decided that the discussion on their plans for the future would take place on his return.

When Dan arrived in Amarillo he went straight to US Marshal Dunhill's office. The marshal was seated at a desk inside, and Dan introduced himself. Dunhill, a spruce, bearded law officer in his fifties, regarded the man in front of him with interest, and invited him to sit down.

'Thanks for getting here so quick,' he said. 'The judge is in town. I'll let him know you're here. I've heard what a good job you did on the Western Cattle Trail. As for the Diamond B, the rangers raided it during the night, and found in Barton's safe some of the proceeds of a recent stagecoach robbery where the driver and one passenger were shot dead by the gang. Then, after they were all in jail, we had a stroke of luck. The Diamond B cook was employed just as a cook on the ranch, but he was scared that just by being there he was in danger of being put in prison for a long spell. He

67

decided to talk. He told us what he had overheard about the criminal activities of the hands while they were talking to one another in the cookshack. So I reckon that most of them will be hanged.

'Now that Matt Barton's been caught,' the marshal went on, 'what are you aiming to do? I ask because I'd like you to take a job as one of my deputy marshals.'

'I appreciate the offer,' said Dan, 'but it don't exactly fit in with some plans I have for the future.'

'I'm disappointed,' said Dunhill, 'but whatever you're plans are, I sure hope they pan out. I'll let you know when the trial's due to start.'

Later in the day Dan was told that the trial would take place the following morning, and he duly attended to give his evidence. At the end of the proceedings, Isaac and Ron Barton, together with three hands, were sentenced to hang. Another two hands, against whom there was no firm evidence that they had been involved in murder, were given medium term prison sentences. The cook was given only a short prison sentence.

On the morning after the trial, Dan set off early for Larraby, and reached the town in the afternoon. He went straight to the store to see Mary, but Warren told him that she had ridden off earlier to visit a close friend of hers, Jane Edison, the young wife of a homesteader, Mark Edison.

She had arranged with Jane to go and talk with her about the plans for her forthcoming wedding. The homestead was about ten miles east of town.

'I figured she'd be back well before now,' said the storekeeper. 'I'm getting a mite worried about her. Looks like she's got held up for some reason.'

'I'll ride out and meet her,' said Dan, and Warren gave him directions to the homestead.

But Dan came in view of the buildings without seeing any sign of Mary. He rode up to the door of the house, dismounted, and knocked on it several times. There was no reply. He opened the door, stepped inside, and pulled up short. On the floor, against a wall, was a man lying motionless, with his eyes closed. Beside him was a woman, tightly bound. Desperately, the woman looked up at Dan. He could see the angry bruise on the side of her face. He guessed that he was looking at Edison and his wife.

Quickly, he moved over to them, and knelt down by the man. He was breathing, but there was a bullet wound in his chest, and he appeared to be unconscious. He turned to the woman, quickly untied her and removed the gag from her mouth. Jane had seen Dan once in Larraby, and she recognized him as the man Mary was about to marry. She sat up, then bent down over her husband. She pulled up his shirt, and looked at the wound. She called out to him several times.

But there was no response. Desperate, she turned to Dan.

'He's in a bad way,' she said. 'I've got to get him to Doc Bellamy.'

'I'll help you,' said Dan, 'but first, has Mary been here?'

'No,' replied Jane. 'I was expecting her, but she never turned up.'

'Right,' said Dan, deeply worried about Mary, and hoping against hope that he would find her in Larraby. 'You put a pad over the wound to stop it bleeding, and hold it there with a bandage. I'll go and hitch up the buckboard.'

It was now dark outside. Twenty minutes later, with Mark Edison lying on a mattress on the floor of the buckboard, and Dan's horse tied behind it, they left the homestead for Larraby. As they drove on through the night, Jane, sitting by the side of her husband, told Dan what had happened at the homestead.

'A couple of hours before Mary was due,' she said, 'a stranger rode up from the east and asked if he could water his horse. He behaved pretty pleasant and polite, and we invited him to take a meal with us. He told us he was an old friend of yours. He asked us if he would find you in Larraby, and we said you were expected back from Amarillo soon. We told him about the wedding, and said if he stayed a little while, he'd have the chance of meeting Mary at the homestead. He said he would wait for her, but then, suddenly, his face changed, and he pulled out a gun, and raised it to pistol-whip Mark on the head. Mark dodged the blow, and came at the stranger. But he didn't stand a chance. He was shot in the chest before he could get close enough to grab the gun. I went to help him, but the stranger punched me on my face, and knocked me out. When I came to he was just finishing tying me up. He took a look at Mark, who hadn't moved, and I guess he figured he was dead, or very near. Then, without saying a word, he left the house, and I didn't see him again. Not long after he had gone I fancied I heard voices outside, but I could have been wrong. And after that, nothing happened till you turned up.'

Just then Mark groaned and moved his head slightly. Jane bent over and spoke to him, but he had relapsed into an unconscious state. She told Dan what had just happened.

'Maybe there's still a chance,' she said. 'Maybe Doc Bellamy will be able to save Mark.'

'I sure hope so,' said Dan. 'I've heard he's a good doctor.'

A few moments later, Dan asked Jane to describe the stranger. She did this in detail, and it soon became clear to Dan that the man she was describing was Matt Barton, who had been scheduled for hanging in Dodge a few days ago.

Greatly alarmed by what he had just heard, Dan wondered how Barton could have escaped the hangman, and whether a mad lust for revenge on himself had driven him to kidnap Mary. As soon as he had handed over the homesteader to the doctor he would immediately check whether Mary had returned to town.

On reaching Larraby they stopped at the doctor's house and Dan helped Bellamy carry the unconscious man inside. Then he hurried to the store, to find that an anxious Warren had not seen his daughter since she left to visit Jane. Deeply worried now, Dan told the storekeeper what had happened at the homestead, and of his belief that it was Matt Barton who had been there.

'It's beginning to look,' he said, 'as though Barton might have kidnapped Mary and ridden off with her. He knew she was visiting the homestead.'

Warren was distraught. 'What can we do?' he asked.

'Not much in the dark,' Dan replied, 'but I'll get a posse together and we'll set off for the Edison homestead two hours before daybreak. We'll search the area, and see what sign we can pick up. But right now, I'm going to find the telegraph operator and give him a message to send to the sheriff in Dodge. I'll ask him to confirm that Matt Barton has escaped.'

'I'll see to the posse,' said Warren. 'You find the

telegraph operator, then see how Edison is doing. I'll see you back at the store.'

Dan found the operator at his house. He handed him the message and asked him to send it as soon as the office opened in the morning. Then he went to the doctor's house, to find that Bellamy had extracted the bullet and his patient was still unconscious, but alive.

'It was a very close call,' said the doctor. 'If the bullet hadn't been deflected just a mite, it would have gone straight into his heart. As it is, I think it's not going to be that long before he's fit again. He should be coming round soon.'

Dan went back to the store, where he was later joined by Warren. The storekeeper told him that he himself, with six townsmen, would be ready to leave town two hours before daybreak.

Shortly after midnight, a torrential rainstorm swept across the area, moving east.

SEVEN

Waiting for the time of their departure, both Dan and Warren were gravely concerned about the plight of Mary, now probably in the hands of a hardened criminal. The posse, with Dan leading it, left town at the appointed time, and headed for the Edison homestead, arriving a little before daybreak. As soon as it was light enough, they started looking for possible tracks of the horses of Mary and Barton leading away from the homestead. But the task was hopeless. A deluge of rain during the night had destroyed any tracks made the previous day.

They carried out an exhaustive search of a wide area around the homestead, but this yielded no sign of Mary. There seemed little doubt that she had been kidnapped, and had ridden off with her captor, in a direction unknown to the posse. When darkness fell, they returned to Larraby, where a telegraph message was waiting for Dan. It was from the sheriff in Dodge City. It read: MATT BARTON ON THE LOOSE. ESCAPED FROM JAIL ALONE KILLING A DEPUTY SHERIFF. BELIEVE HE CROSSED INTO THE INDIAN TERRITORY. SHERIFF DAWSON DODGE CITY.

Dan showed the message to Warren.

'This clinches it,' he said. 'Matt Barton has Mary. I'm remembering the way he was looking at me when I was giving evidence against him in Dodge City. I reckon he might have taken Mary to help him get hold of me. I think that probably Mary's safe for now. I reckon Barton's aiming to get in touch with me soon.'

'I'm worried sick about Mary,' said the storekeeper. 'What can we do to get her back?'

'I feel just the same as you do,' said Dan, 'but we have no idea where she's being held. It's not going to be easy, but I think we should wait till we hear from Barton.'

'I guess you're right,' said Warren.

They did not have long to wait. The following morning a homesteader who was working a quarter section some way north of the Edison place drove his buckboard into town and handed over a sealed envelope addressed to Dan, and marked GET THIS TO THE MARSHAL. URGENT.

'This was slipped under the door of the house during the night,' said the homesteader, 'and seeing as you'd called yesterday looking for Mary, I figured it might be important.'

Dan thanked him, then opened the envelope, and took out the letter inside. It read: I HAVE THE WOMAN BUT IT'S YOU I WANT KINCAID. SHE'LL BE FREED UNHARMED IF YOU RIDE EAST AND ALONE TO EAGLE BLUFF JUST INSIDE INDIAN TERRITORY AND GIVE YOURSELF UP TO THE MEN WAITING THERE. IF ANYBODY IS SEEN FOLLOWING YOU THE WOMAN DIES. AND IF YOU BRING IN THE LAW TO HELP YOU THE WOMAN DIES. ARRIVE AT EAGLE BLUFF AT NOON TOMORROW THURSDAY. MATT BARTON.

Dan left his office and went to see Warren at the store. He showed him the letter.

'I'm certain Barton's threats are real,' said Dan. 'Killing a woman in cold blood wouldn't bother him one bit. The only way to save Mary is to do exactly as Barton says. And even then we can't be sure he'll let Mary go. I think, in Mary's interests, it's best if we keep this between our two selves for the time being. I know where Eagle Bluff is. I passed it when I was following the Diamond B hands to the Western Cattle Trail. I'll leave here at noon, and camp out a while on the trail. I've got to be sure of turning up at Eagle Bluff at noon tomorrow.'

'I suppose,' said the storekeeper, 'that there's no doubt that Barton means to kill you?'

'No doubt at all,' said Dan, 'probably with a spell of torture thrown in first. But I've always figured that until the last breath has been drawn, there's always a chance of turning the tables. It's all a matter of being ready to seize that chance when it crops up. I know all this is pretty hard on you. I'm hoping Mary will turn up here two or three days from now.'

Dan left at noon, and camped out for a while during the night at a point not far west of the border with the Indian Territory. He resumed his journey after daybreak, at a time which would allow him to reach his destination by noon. He crossed the border, and before long he caught sight of Eagle Bluff in the far distance. It stood in the middle of a large expanse of level ground. As he headed towards it he felt sure that he was being observed from the bluff and possibly from other points in the area.

As he reached the bluff two men holding six-guns stepped out from a recess in the side, and ordered him to stop and dismount. One of the men Dan recognized instantly as Matt Barton. The other man, Massey, was a stranger to Dan. He was the leader of a gang of three outlaws with whom Barton had worked occasionally in the past. On escaping from the jail in Dodge City, Barton had ridden to a ravine in the Indian Territory, not far south of the Kansas border, where he knew Massey and his men Delaney and Carter were hiding out.

On the promise of a rich reward to be funded by the proceeds, hidden in a secret place, of past robberies carried out by Barton, the outlaws agreed to help him in his determination to wreak vengeance on the man who had caused the downfall of himself and his father and brother.

At the time that Dan was confronted by Barton and Massey, Carter was watching the trail from the west, to make sure that nobody was following Dan. Delaney, the third member of the gang, was holding Mary in a gully a few miles to the east.

At the bluff, Dan's weapons were taken from him and he was searched. Then Barton regarded him with grim satisfaction and a mad lust for revenge.

'I was sure you'd turn up, Kincaid,' he said. 'I knew that a man like you would have to give himself up to save his bride-to-be. . . .'

'Where is she?' asked Dan. 'I've given myself up on the understanding that you let her go. She's done nothing to harm you. If you leave her at the nearest town, she'll be able to get back to Larraby.'

'The woman's not far away,' said Barton. 'You two will soon be together again. But what a fool you are, Kincaid. You never really expected me to free the woman, did you? I have better plans for her.' He grinned evilly before continuing. 'I've lost a father and brother because of you. It only seems fair you should lose the woman you were aiming to get hitched to. Before you die yourself, you'll see her die in front of your eyes. And she won't die easy.'

'I knew you'd sunk pretty far, Barton,' said Dan,

'but it never crossed my mind that you'd sunk so low as to torture and kill a woman who'd done you no harm.'

Barton's only reaction was a broad grin. He ordered Dan on to his horse. Then he and Massey mounted, and with Massey leading Dan's mount, the three riders headed east, towards the place where Mary was being held.

When she saw Dan, hands bound, riding up the gully towards her accompanied by Barton and Massey, Mary's heart sank. Her hope had been that Dan would find some way of rescuing her. Barton stopped in front of Mary.

'See what a nice surprise we have here for you,' he said. 'I reckon you two have a lot to talk about.'

Soon Dan and Mary, hands and feet bound, were seated side by side on the ground with their backs against a large boulder standing near the side of the gully. Their three captors were seated nearby. They were awaiting the arrival of Carter.

Dan spoke to Mary by his side. She looked fairly composed, but he could sense the fear that was gripping her.

'Have they harmed you, Mary?' he asked.

'Not so far,' she said, with a tremor in her voice, 'but Barton told me he had something special in store for me when you came along. What are they going to do with us, Dan?'

'It's pretty clear,' Dan replied, 'that our

prospects ain't that good. Barton knows I'm responsible for bringing him and his father and brother to trial. He's out for revenge. And he reckons to include you because we're close enough to be fixing to get married.'

'Is there anything we can do?' asked Mary, desperately.

'There's always a chance while we're still alive,' said Dan, 'and it looks like Barton ain't ready to finish us off just yet.'

As he stopped speaking Carter rode in, to report that he was sure that no one had been following Dan. Barton walked over to the prisoners. He grinned down at them.

'You'll be interested to hear,' he said, 'that you ain't going to die here. It's too close to the Texas Panhandle for my liking. We're moving east to a safer place before we start work on you two.'

Soon they were all riding to the east, and Dan and Mary were unable to talk further. It was around midnight when they reached the ravine where the Massey gang had been hiding out. In it was a small long-abandoned shack in which the gang had been sleeping. They rode up to it and dismounted.

'We'll 'tend to these two after daybreak,' said Barton. 'I'm ready for some sleep.'

'They'll have to stay outside the shack,' said Massey. 'There's only room to sleep three in there.'

'All right,' said Barton, 'but we need to have a

man outside guarding them. And make sure they're tied up good.'

A fire was lit a little way from the shack, The prisoners were ordered to lie on the ground not far from the fire. Their legs were tightly bound, and it was confirmed that their wrists were tightly roped together in front of them. Carter was selected for the first spell of night guard duty, and after he and the others had swallowed a drink of coffee, he sat down close to the fire, with his back to a boulder, and facing the two prisoners. The other three outlaws disappeared into the shack.

As far as Dan was concerned there was still a glimmer of hope. Before leaving Larraby he had been to see Doc Bellamy, and had taken him into his confidence about his forthcoming appointment at the bluff. Bellamy had supplied him with a small surgical knife, slender and razor-sharp. Then he called in a widowed lady along the street who, among other things, carried out clothing repairs. At the back of Dan's shirt, where it was normally covered by the wide belt holding up his trousers, she sewed on a small horizontal pocket which snugly accommodated the knife, leaving the end of the handle protruding slightly. With the belt and shirt in their normal positions, the knife was completely hidden.

Lying close to Mary on the ground at the outlaws' hideout, Dan told her about the knife. Their whispered conversation was inaudible to Carter.

'I'm going to lie with my back to you,' said Dan. 'If you pull up the shirt from inside the belt, you should be able to take out the knife. But it's mighty sharp. Take care not to cut yourself.'

Within minutes, Mary had the knife in her hand. Her movements had been so slight that, in the gloom, they were not noticed by Carter.

'I'm holding the knife,' whispered Mary. 'What now?'

'I'm going to turn over to face you,' whispered Dan. 'The way that rope around my wrist is knotted, it ain't possible for you to undo the knot with your hands tied. But you can use the knife to cut through the rope. And once you've freed my hands, the rest is easy. Just feel for the rope with your fingers, then saw across it with the blade of the knife. And keep as still as you can.'

Dan rolled over to face Mary. She positioned herself, then started sawing on the rope. The slight movement of her hands and arms was not visible to the guard. The keen blade of the knife, in Mary's slender supple hand, soon sliced through the rope, and Dan felt his hands come free. Quickly, he took the knife from Mary's hand and cut through the rope around her wrists.

'So far, so good,' whispered Dan, 'but he's going to spot us if we start freeing our legs. I guess he's tired. I'm praying he's going to doze off before long.'

Dan's prayer was answered. Twenty minutes later they saw that Carter's head had slumped forward and the faint sound of a snore was heard through the still night air. Dan sat up and leaned forward to start cutting through the rope around his legs. He froze as the snoring suddenly ceased, and he quickly assumed his previous position, lying on the ground. He hid the knife underneath him, then both he and Mary rewound the length of rope around their wrists to give the impression that they were still tied.

They heard Carter coughing for a short spell, then he lit a cigarette, rose to his feet, and walked over to the two prisoners. He looked down at them briefly, then returned to his previous position and sat down again. Soon the cigarette end was thrown to the ground; five minutes later Carter's head slumped forward and he began to snore.

'We'll wait a few minutes,' whispered Dan, 'then I'll put Carter out of action, and take his gun. Then we'll take him and the three men in the shack prisoner. Are you game, Mary?'

She nodded. 'I'm game,' she said. 'I'll help you as much as I can.'

After a short wait Dan sat up again. Working as fast as he could, he cut the rope binding his legs, then did the same for Mary. They both stood up, and Dan looked round hurriedly for a stone or a piece of rock with which he could knock the guard unconscious while he was still dozing. But he had not yet found anything suitable when the snoring abruptly cease. Carter coughed, his head lifted, and his eyes opened.

The guard's reaction was quick. He could see, through the darkness, the upright figures of Dan and Mary. He pulled out his six-gun and started firing towards them. As soon as Dan realized that Carter was awake, he grabbed Mary's hand. They stooped and ran off away from the guard, dodging and twisting, and almost immediately they were out of his sight. Although two of the shots came very close to them, the couple had the good fortune to remain unscathed. They ran up the ravine, and climbed out of it, to stand on the level ground at the top.

'We've got to get as far away from here as we can before daybreak,' said Dan. 'Then we'll have to find a good place to hide. Those four will be scouring the area for us as soon as it's light.'

Dan headed south, a direction chosen at random, since he was not familiar with the surrounding area. They set off at a slow run, which eventually reduced to a walk as their strength ebbed away. Coming to a small brook which ran across their path, they were able to slake their thirst. They had travelled about six miles, and dawn was not far away, when they saw, looming in front of them, a large rock outcrop. They ran round the base, and on the far side they stopped.

'They'll be out looking for us soon,' said Dan. 'Considering the sort of ground we've just passed over, and the fact that we're on foot, they're going to find it hard to follow our tracks. I think we should look round here for a good place to hide till nightfall.'

They walked along the foot of the outcrop, and came to a large tall patch of brush growing against the wall. It was light enough now for Dan to examine this. He pushed his way inside, and emerged a few minutes later.

'Behind the brush,' he told Mary, 'there's a small cave. We'll stay in there till nightfall. But before we go in there we'll rest a little while, then take a quick look at the area around here.'

Shortly after, walking round the outcrop, they came in sight of a large grove of trees, with a clear space of seventy yards between it and the outcrop.

'Let's take a very quick look at that,' said Dan, 'before we go into hiding.'

Just as they were about to move away from the wall against which they were standing, Dan glanced towards the north, then shrank back, taking Mary with him. In the far distance, only just visible, he could see four riders, one of them well in front of the others, slowly approaching them, seemingly along the path which Dan and Mary had trod earlier.

'That's Barton and the others, for sure,' said Dan. 'The one in front must be a real first-class tracker. Let's hurry. We ain't got much time.'

He broke off part of a small bush growing close by, then used it to obliterate their tracks as they walked backwards to the cave. Then, working on the side of the outcrop remote from the approaching riders, he and Mary hastily obliterated some of their tracks, and made some new ones. When they had finished, their footprints stopped at the foot of the outcrop, at a point a little under twenty yards from the cave, giving the impression that the couple had climbed up on to the outcrop, whose size and nature was such that many hiding places would be available there. Before entering the cave, they closed the brush behind them.

Ten minutes later they heard the faint sound of voices outside. Carefully parting the brush, Dan loked out. He saw four horses near the point where the tracks ended. Standing by the horses were Barton and the Massey gang. As he watched, Delaney mounted his horse and rode off on a circuit of the outcrop, eventually returning, past the concealed cave entrance, to the others. Dan assumed that he had been checking for tracks leading away from the outcrop. Barton and Massey started to climb it. They were followed by Delaney, whose experience as a scout in the army had kept them so hard on the heels of their quarry. Carter stayed behind, standing near the horses. Dan retreated into the cave. He told Mary what he had seen.

'I was hoping,' he said, 'that they would leave the horses picketed, and all four would climb up to search for us. Then we could have taken all their mounts, and got clear away. We'll have to leave here before they find out we're not hiding up there. We'll try to get to that grove of trees without any of them spotting us.'

He left the cave and looked out through the brush again. This time, he could see that Carter was seated on the ground, close to the horses. His back was to the wall. He was wearing a holstered six-gun, and was holding a rifle across his legs. He was facing in such a direction that the brush was within his field of vision. Dan went into the cave.

'There's a chance,' he told Mary, 'that we can slip away without Carter seeing us, if we can manage to divert his attention. I thought of trying to rush him and knocking him out so's we could escape with the horses, but I just couldn't get near enough without him seeing me. It would be too risky. Let's do it this way.'

After a brief discussion with Mary, Dan looked round the floor of the cave, and found a few small pieces of rock, which he pocketed. Then he led the way out of the cave and, with Mary crouching by his side, he peered out at Carter. The outlaw was still sitting in the same position, and remained so, without moving, for the next ten minutes. Then he reached in his vest pocket for the makings, and quickly rolled a cigarette. But just as he finished this, it fell from his hand in to the grass by his leg. As he bent down to retrieve it, Dan straightened up for a moment and threw a piece of rock, aiming at the horses. Too small to do any real harm, it struck the nearest horse on the flank.

The animal reared, then ran off for a short distance. Cursing, Carter rose and followed it. While he was so engaged, Dan and Mary left the brush and ran along the curving side of the outcrop. By the time Carter had retrieved the horse, they were out of his sight. They moved round until they were opposite the grove of trees, then headed for it, praying they would not be seen byy any of the men searching for them above.

Good fortune was with them. They entered the grove and ran through it to the far side. Emerging at the only point not visible from the outcrop, they found themselves standing on the almost sheer bank of a fast-flowing river running across their path. It was flowing through flat terrain, and the top of the bank was about nine feet above the surface of the water. Dan looked around, assessing the situation.

'There's only one way we can get away from

here, without the danger of them spotting us, Mary,' he said, 'and that's to get in the water and float downstream. I reckon it'll be a while before they find out we've given them the slip, and follow our tracks down here. By that time we need to be as far away from here as we can get. How d'you feel about floating in the water?'

Mary tried to conceal her fear of the ordeal ahead of them.

'I ain't had much practice,' she said, 'but I'll be all right.'

'Just take a deep breath before you hit the water,' said Dan. 'Relax when you come up, and lie on your back. I'll help to keep you afloat. Let's go.'

Hand in hand, they took a short run up to the top of the bank and jumped out, to fall into the deep water below. Soon they were floating downstream together. The water was cool, but not uncomfortably so.

On the outcrop, with its numerous possible hiding-places, the three outlaws continued to search for them.

EIGHT

Eight miles downstream from the point where Dan and Mary had jumped into the water, two elderly prospectors, Hank Potter and Nat Mooney, were taking a well-earned break by the side of the river. At the point where they were seated the top of the river bank was still well above water level. A little way downstream a few yards of the bank had collapsed and fallen into the water.

Hank and Nat had become partners many years earlier while prospecting in California, and had stayed together ever since. They had moved on to Nevada and Colorado, but the find that was to make them rich had so far eluded them. Now, spurred on by a firm belief that their luck was bound to turn one day, they had gone into the Indian Territory in the hope that they might find, in some unexpected place, what they had been seeking for so many years.

Hank drained the last few drops from a large mug of coffee. As he put the mug down he glanced upstream. Something was floating downriver towards them. A moment later he realized that he was looking at two people in the water, one supporting the other.

'Nat!' he yelled, pointing to the two people in the water. Rising to his feet, he grabbed a coil of rope lying on the ground nearby, and ran up to the top of the bank. Dan, almost abreast by now, and with his strength failing fast, saw Hank. The prospector ran along the bank and threw one end of the rope down to Dan, who grabbed it. Keeping pace with Dan and Mary, Hank pulled them into the side, and they brought up against the mass of debris lying where the bank had collapsed. He held them there while Nat clambered down and helped them out of the water. Soon they were sitting, exhausted, near the campfire on which the prospectors had cooked their recent meal.

Dan looked up at the two men who had come to their aid. They were both short and slim, weather-beaten and bearded. Although not related, they could easily have been taken for twins. Quickly, Dan told them how they came to be in the river.

'Before long,' he went on, 'I'm expecting those four outlaws to be riding past here, along the bank, looking for us. They're a mean bunch, and I wouldn't want you two to get hurt. Is there anywhere round here where we could hide safe till they've gone by?'

'I know just the spot,' Hank replied. 'It's inside the cave there.'

He pointed to the entrance to a cave at the foot of a nearby hill. 'That's where we're looking round for gold right now. I'll take you there. But first you've got to get those wet clothes off, dry yourselves, and put on some spare clothes of ours. It's clear they ain't going to fit that well, but that can't be helped. The lady can change behind the burros over there. And while you're doing that, Nat will climb that knoll over there, and watch out for riders coming this way along the river bank.'

'We're mighty obliged,' said Dan. He and Mary quickly undressed, dried themselves, and put on the clothes given them by Hank. Carrying the wet clothes, they followed Hank into the cave, which was large, and roughly circular. One passage led off it, but this came to a dead end after fifteen feet. After lighting a lamp Hank led them into this passage and pointed to a hole, roughly circular and about two feet in diameter, at the top of the side wall. The bottom of the hole was eleven feet from the floor of the passage. A makeshift ladder was standing nearby.

'That's your hiding-place,' said Hank. 'That hole up there leads to a passage that stops about twenty feet in. There's plenty of room for you two to lie in there, end to end. Climb up into it, and I'll push these wet clothes in after you. We'll dry them later. I'll take the ladder out with me and hide it. I'll be back to let you know when they've gone.'

'Right,' said Dan. 'One thing, though. They've got an expert tracker with them. You'd better wipe out any of our tracks between here and the river.'

I'll do that,' said Hank, and watched as Dan, then Mary, climbed up into the passage, and disappeared from view. After pushing their wet clothes in after them, he took the ladder outside and hid it, before effacing the tracks of Dan and Mary. Then he sat down to wait.

It was a further half-hour before Nat came running back to tell him that four riders were approaching. They both sat by the fire, and only rose when Barton and the others rode up to them.

The four riders dismounted and Delaney moved around, looking at the ground for tracks. Barton walked up to the two prospectors.

'We're chasing a couple of bank robbers,' he said curtly. 'A man and a woman. Figured they might have floated downstream. Happen you've seen them?'

'Ain't never heard of a female bank robber before,' said Hank. 'Women just don't know their place nowadays. But if you're lawmen, why don't I see any badges?'

'There's no time to explain,' said Barton, testily.

'Did you see the man and woman?'

'They could've floated by without us seeing them,' said Hank. 'We've been in the cave over there for three hours or so. Figured we might find gold somewhere in there. Only came out half an hour ago.'

Barton looked at Delaney, who had just joined them. Delaney shook his head. Barton turned to the two prospectors.

'We'll be on our way,' he said, 'but first, we'll take a look inside the cave. Have you got a lamp?'

'There's one on the floor inside,' said Hank. Barton and Delaney made a brief inspection of the cave before riding on downriver with the others.

Waiting until the outlaws were out of sight, and leaving Nat on watch, Hank took the ladder into the cave, and came out shortly with Dan and Mary. Their clothes were put by the fire to dry, and they were given food and drink.

'How far is the nearest town?' asked Dan, as they were eating the meal.

'About twelve miles to the south,' said Hank. 'Indian Rock, it's called. We dropped in there a couple of weeks ago. They have a hotel, and a store and livery stable.'

'I think we'll head there right now,' said Dan. 'Maybe Barton and the others will come back this way when they can't find us. The sooner we can get to Indian Rock, the better.'

'You're right,' said Hank, 'and to make it sooner, you'd best ride there on the two mules. We won't be needing them for a while. When you get to Indian Rock you can get somebody to bring them back here. I guess the liveryman will arrange that for you. The other thing is, you're going to need some cash. We ain't exactly flush, but we can loan you enough for you to get by till you can pay us back.'

Dan and Mary thanked the two prospectors, and left them ten minutes later. They reached Indian Rock without incident. Their first call was at the livery stable. Garner, the liveryman, eyed them with considerable curiosity. He thought he recognized the two mules. Dan briefly explained how he and Mary cane to be riding them, and he asked Garner if he could have them taken back to the owners.

'Sure,' said the liveryman. 'I'll get that done tomorrow.'

Dan asked whether Garner knew of any lawmen in the area.

'You're in luck,' said the liveryman. 'They ain't turned up yet, but I heard that two deputy US marshals would likely be calling here today or tomorrow.'

'Good,' said Dan. 'We're going to the hotel now. If you see them ride in, would you ask them to see us there? Tell them it's real urgent. And we need a couple of horses. Can you help us with that?'

I'll loan you two,' said Garner, 'and be glad to. And I'm bound to see the deputies when they ride into town. I'll tell them what you said.'

They thanked the liveryman and went to the hotel, where they took two rooms. A little later they went into the dining room for supper. They were just finishing their meal when two deputy US marshals, Larkin and Norton, walked into the room, looked round, and came up to their table. They were both tough, capable-looking men in their middle forties, with many years of experience upholding the law in the Indian Territory, which often provided a haven for outlaws fleeing from the law after committing criminal offences in the surrounding states.

'You Kincaid?' asked Norton.

Dan nodded. 'We're sure glad to see you two,' he said. 'Sit down, and I'll tell you just why.'

He gave them an account of recent events, to which the two deputies listened with interest.

'We heard about Miss Warren being kidnapped, and how you had gone into the Indian Territory to look for her,' said Norton. 'You say that a man called Massey, and two others with him, are helping Matt Barton. We knew that the Massey gang was hiding somewhere in the territory, but not where.'

'We can take you to the hideout,' said Dan. 'It

ain't that far from here. If Barton figures we're both drowned, the gang could have gone back to their hideout, and maybe Barton with them.'

'Could be,' said Norton. 'We'll ride there with you first thing tomorrow.'

'I'll get me some weapons and ammunition before we leave,' said Dan. 'And I'll take the two mules back to the prospectors. Maybe they saw Barton and the others again after we'd left.'

Dan went to see the liveryman, to tell him they would be leaving with the deputies in the morning, and would take the mules with them. He asked Garner how he could get a message to Mary's father in Larraby to say that she and Dan were now safe, and were helping the law to catch up with Garner and the men who had been helping him.

'Leave the message with me,' said the liveryman. 'I'll make sure it gets there, probably about two days from now.'

Early the following morning, Dan and Mary rode out of town with the two deputies.

NINE

When Barton and the others left the two prospectors, they continued along the riverbank for two hours without seeing any sign of Dan and Mary. Then they came to a halt.

'No point in riding any further,' said Barton. 'They must have drowned. That water's pretty deep. Their bodies will be miles downstream by now. Let's go back to the hideout.'

They turned, and rode back along the bank upstream. When they reached the prospectors' camp, they saw Nat and Hank standing near the cave entrance, but ignored them, and continued on their way.

'Looks like they've given up the search,' said Hank. 'I'll climb that knoll, and watch them till they're out of sight.'

He watched from the knoll as the four riders continued steadily along the riverbank in the growing darkness. They were almost out of sight, and he was preparing to leave the knoll, when he saw them stop. A few minutes later, they all turned, and started riding back towards the camp. Hastily, Hank returned to Nat.

'I don't like it, Nat,' he said. 'They're coming back. Why in tarnation would they do that? I've got a bad feeling about it. I reckon we should find a place to hide from them, and we ain't got much time. They were moving pretty fast in this direction. One thing, it's getting darker all the time.'

'How about that big patch of thick brush along the hillside?' asked Nat. 'If we go right now, we can get there without them seeing us.'

'A good idea,' said Hank. He hurried to pick up an old shotgun and a bag of cartridges lying on the ground near the burros. Then they both ran over a hundred yards to the brush patch, and disappeared inside it, leaving no indication behind them that it had recently been disturbed.

When Hank saw the four riders suddenly come to a halt in the distance they were following the example of Delaney, who was in the lead, and who had suddenly reined in his mount.

'What's wrong?' asked Massey.

'It just struck me,' said Delaney, 'that when we were talking to those two prospectors a few hours

99

ago, I saw two mules and two burros nearby. But when we rode past just now, the two mules weren't there.'

'They could've been grazing somewhere out of sight,' said Barton, 'but we'd best make sure. Let's ride back there.'

In the gathering darkness they rode towards the camp. Delaney went on ahead to circle the camp, looking for the mules. He joined the others as they stopped near the campfire.

'No sign of the mules,' he said, 'and them two prospectors don't seem to be anywhere around either. Maybe they're inside the cave over there.'

'Let's take a look,' said Barton, and the others followed him to the cave. It was dark inside, and they lit an oil lamp which was standing on the floor. It was soon clear that there was nobody in the cave or the passage leading off it. In the passage Barton noticed a ladder standing against the wall, which had not been there at the time of their previous inspection. He held the lamp up high, and saw the hole at the top of the wall. Delaney climbed the ladder to take a look at the hole, and disappeared from view. He reappeared a little later, to report that there was plenty of room behind the hole for two people to hide in.

'Damnation!' shouted Barton. 'We've been tricked. It looks like Kincaid and the woman were here all the time. I'm guessing that as soon as we left, they rode off on the mules, probably to Indian Rock. That means we could be on the run ourselves pretty soon. We'd better leave here right now.'

'We can't stay on at the hideout,' said Massey, 'now that Kincaid knows where it is.'

'You're right,' said Barton, 'but I know another place not far off, where we can stay till they've stopped looking for us. And then I'll go after Kincaid on my own. I'd like to deal with those two prospectors who helped to trick us, but we ain't got the time to look for them. Let's go.'

They mounted, and rode off to collect some items from the hideout. When they reached the ravine, they took a quick meal, while reviewing the situation. Delaney mentioned that on visits he had paid to Indian Rock from the hideout for supplies in the past, he had heard that deputy US marshals called regularly at the town.

'Just in case Kincaid has managed to get help from the law,' said Barton, 'and they're close on our heels, I think we should head towards Kansas. We'll stop about ten miles from here. I reckon Delaney should stay behind here in hiding to see *if* the law is on our heels. When he finds out, one way or the other, he can hightail it to the place where we're waiting. Then we can decide whether to go to a hideout east of here, or head for Kansas. Any deputy US marshals following us will have to stop at the border.'

This was agreed, and Barton rode off to the north with Massey and Carter, leaving Delaney behind.

The following morning, when Dan and Mary, with the two deputies, arrived at the prospectors' camp, Hank told them what had happened the previous evening.

'My guess is,' he concluded, 'that they suspected you'd been here, and came back to look round. I figure they noticed the two mules were missing, and it's likely they spotted the place where you were hiding. They didn't stay here long, and we think they rode off to the east.'

'I suppose they could've gone back to Massey's hideout,' said Norton, 'to pick up anything they might have left there. I reckon we should ride straight there and find out.'

Dan turned to Mary. 'On second thoughts, Mary,' he said, 'maybe you should go back to Indian Rock, and wait there for me. Those are four real dangerous men we're after.'

'I don't want to go back,' she said, 'now that we're so close, and the law has taken charge. I have my own score to settle with Barton. I've got the six-gun you bought me in Indian Rock. Maybe I can help. And don't think I'm going to change my mind.'

'All right,' said Dan. A few minutes later they took their leave of Hank and Nat and set off to follow the shortest route to the Massey hideout.

They approached it with caution, but it was soon clear that the four outlaws were not in the ravine. Deputy Larkin who, according to his partner, was a tracker of no mean ability, went on ahead to look at the sign inside the ravine.

While Larkin was doing this Delaney left his hiding-place, from which he had been looking down into the ravine through field glasses, and rode off, unobserved, to the north. He had recognized Dan and Mary, and had seen the lawmen's badges. When he reached the place where Barton and the others were waiting he told them what he had seen.

Barton cursed. 'We'll have to cross the border into Kansas,' he said. 'The deputies will have to give up the chase there. But maybe Kincaid and the woman will cross into Kansas, with the idea of setting the law on us there. What we'll do is wait in hiding on the other side of the border, and kill them both after they've crossed.'

Back at the ravine, when Larkin returned to the others, he told them that a number of men, at least three, had been in the ravine around twelve hours ago, and had ridden off to the north.

'It'll be slow going,' he said, 'but I reckon I can

follow those tracks till nightfall. We'd better get started. They could be heading for the Kansas border.'

They made camp five miles north of the ravine, and continued following the tracks at daybreak. Well after midday they reached the border with Kansas, marked by a weather-beaten signpost by the side of the trail, and stopped. Norton spoke to Dan and Mary.

'I'm sorry,' he said, 'but this is as far as we can go. Are you two aiming to keep up the chase?'

'When Mary was kidnapped,' said Dan, 'we were fixing to get married. I reckon we should go ahead with that, and leave the law to deal with Barton and the others. It was different before I met Mary. Then I had only one thing on my mind. And that was to catch up with Matt Barton and hand him over to the law. Now things are different. What do *you* think, Mary?'

Mary nodded her head. 'I was hoping you'd say that,' she said.

'There's a chance Barton will decide to come after us again,' said Dan, 'but that's a chance we'll have to take.'

'I reckon you're doing the right thing,' said Norton. 'You can ride back with us to Indian Rock. I'll make sure that the lawmen in Kansas are told that Barton and the others have crossed into the state.'

Watching through field glasses from the cover of a small grove of trees just north of the border, Barton cursed as he saw Dan and Mary ride off to the south with the two deputies. He spoke to Massey, by his side.

'I reckon we should stay in hiding in Kansas for a short while,' he said, 'before we go back into the Indian Territory.'

When Dan and Mary arrived back in Larraby Mary's father was greatly relieved. They told him of the escape of Barton over the border into Kansas, and of their intention to go ahead with the wedding. Mary's father told them that he had heard that a reward was due to Dan for his part in the the capture of the whole Barton gang. He also said that the Diamond B was to be sold by the state, the proceeds to go towards reimbursing victims of the gang's criminal activities. Then he left them, to go into the store.

'Now we can have that talk about our future,' said Dan. 'First, tell me what ideas you have in mind.'

'There's two things I don't want,' said Mary. 'First, I wouldn't want to be living too far away from my father. And second, I know you were a lawman in Colorado, but I don't think that's a job for a married man who's on the way to having a family to raise.'

'That's fine by me,' said Dan. 'I only took the deputy sheriff job in Colorado for Miriam's sake. I liked the job of running my father's cattle ranch. If we could find a cattle ranch for sale somewhere near here, how would that suit you, Mary?'

'I think that would suit me very well,' said Mary. 'How about the Diamond B?'

'Just what I was thinking,' said Dan. 'With the reward money, and the money I got from selling the ranch in Colorado, we should have enough to clinch the deal. I'll find out who's managing the sale. If we're lucky enough to end up with the ranch, we'll start off in a small way, and build up a sizeable herd.'

Two weeks later, Dan and Mary were married, and three days after that, the purchase of the Diamond B, with a small herd of cattle which had been left there when Isaac Barton, with his son Ron and the hands had been taken into custody, was completed.

'Now we've got to find some ranch hands,' said Dan to Mary. 'And maybe that ain't going to be easy. Three or four should do to start with.'

But they were in luck. Three cowboys, who had been signed on to help drive a trail herd from south Texas to Wyoming, called at the store on their way back. Having no jobs to go back to, they asked Warren if they might find work at any of the ranches in the area. The storekeeper took them to

Dan and Mary, who were in the living quarters. While talking to them for a while, Dan took a liking to the three men, who were obviously close friends. He offered them jobs on the Diamond B, after giving them a brief account of his recent clash with Matt Barton. He told them that there was just a possibility that if the law did not catch up with him, Barton might still be out for revenge. The three men accepted his offer and, taking some provisions from the store, they and Dan rode out to the ranch, where they found that the bunkhouse and cookshack needed very little attention to lick them into shape.

Before riding back to Larraby Dan told the three men to ride on to the range and check on the location and condition of the cattle. He told them that he and Mary would be moving out to the ranch in a few days. When he had departed for Larraby, the three hands, Ewing, Flint and Gummer, pleased that they had found work with what they judged to be a good employer, settled down to familiarize themselves with the ranch, and see to all the chores that the work involved.

TEN

A week after the three hands started work at the ranch, Mary and Dan moved in and set about fixing up the ranch house to their liking.

The cattle turned out to be in good condition, and there was plenty of good grazing on the range. Dan was pleased with the work of the three hands. They were all strong healthy men in their thirties. Jim Ewing was short and stocky, an optimist, with a joke never far from his lips. By contrast, Jesse Flint topped six feet, was slim in build, and had a more serious attitude to life. Joe Gummer, average in height and build, was a placid man and a slow thinker but, like the other two, he was an experienced cowhand and utterly dependable. Dan counted himself lucky to have them on his payroll. A cook was needed, but until one could be found Mary was providing meals in the cookshack for everyone.

They had not been long at the ranch when Mary told Dan that she suspected she was pregnant. They were both overjoyed when this was confirmed later by Doc Bellamy in Larraby. Shortly after this, they managed to hire a cook called Harley, a man known and recommended by Flint.

On the Diamond B all continued to go well. Mary and Dan were looking forward to the birth of their child, and the work on the ranch was progressing smoothly. Dan's intention was to hold a round-up in the spring, at which new calves would be branded and mature beef would be selected for handing over to drovers who would trail the cattle to Dodge City, where they would be taken over by a buyer from the East. Dan then intended to buy some brood stock to increase the size of his herd, and take on more hands.

A few months before the round-up, Dan got some news of Matt Barton in a message from the US marshal in Amarillo, who knew of Dan's part in the capture of the Bartons, and of the kidnapping of Mary. The message told how Matt Barton had been located in the Indian Territory, and that deputies had been sent to capture him. But once again he had escaped. He was believed to have been seriously wounded, and to have gone into hiding somewhere in Arkansas, where the law was actively searching for him.

The baby, a healthy boy, was born just after the

spring round-up, with the help of Doc Bellamy and a woman friend of Mary's from Larraby. Three months after the birth a man called Naylor rode up to the Diamond B, looking for work as a ranch hand. He told Dan that he had been working as a trail hand, but hankered after a more settled job, with the comforts of a bunkhouse. He produced a scrawled letter of recommendation, which read: 'Pete Naylor is a good cowhand. Works hard and never gave me no trouble. Lon Jackson, Trail Boss.'

Naylor gave the impression of being a likeable character, who would get on well with Flint and the others. In need of more hands, Dan decided to take Naylor on for a trial period. He told him this, and took him to meet the other hands.

Over the following week Dan had no complaints about Naylor's work. He decided to offer him a permanent job if he maintained the same standard during the coming week. Towards the end of this period Flint and Naylor carried some furniture up the stairs to baby William's bedroom, which was adjacent to that of his parents.

That evening Naylor rode into Larraby with Gummer, who went straight to the saloon. After buying a few things at the store, Naylor joined Gummer in the saloon for a few drinks. An hour later, Gummer suggested that it was time to ride back to the ranch.

'You go ahead, Joe,' said Naylor. 'There ain't much I like more than a good game of poker. I aim to get into that game over there. I've got a few dollars to spare from my last job, and I've got a feeling tonight might be my lucky night. If I find I'm on a winning streak, don't expect me back at the ranch till long after you and the others have turned in.'

But after Gummer's departure, Naylor made no effort to join in the poker game. He remained at the bar, and a man called Mason, who was standing further along the bar, moved up to him. Showing no sign that they were acquainted, he started a casual conversation with Naylor. Then, as the barkeep moved along the bar out of earshot, the tone of the conversation changed.

'You got the buggy?' asked, Naylor.

'It's waiting outside,' said Mason. 'I told the liveryman I wanted to hire it for a couple of days to look around the area.'

'Good,' said Naylor. 'Drive the buggy a mile south of town, with your own horse tied behind, and wait for me there. I'll be along in half an hour.'

Mason walked out of the saloon. He was a short man, strongly built, with a mean look about him. When Naylor joined him south of town they headed for the Diamond B. It was just before one in the morning when they stopped short of the ranch buildings. Naylor dismounted, and told Mason to wait there for him, ready for a quick getaway.

Naylor walked towards the ranch house. The only light he could see inside it was a very faint one showing through a window in the passage outside the bedrooms. He walked cautiously up to the door of the house and tried the handle. The door was locked on the inside. He walked to a side window and, with a skill born of practice and a minimum of noise, he forced it open with a jemmy and climbed through into the living room. He walked to the door leading to the outside, and unlocked it. Then he tiptoed to the bottom of the stairs. Looking up, he could see a faint light coming from the passage above.

He drew back as he heard the sudden sound of a baby crying upstairs. The sound woke Mary, and the intruder heard her go into the baby's bedroom to comfort the child. Soon the crying stopped, and he heard Mary return to her room. He waited a short while, then started to climb up the stairs, slowly and carefully. He paused with both feet on the eighth step from the bottom, then bypassed the ninth step which had produced an exceptionally loud creak when he had stepped on it during the previous day. At the top of the stairs he paused again. A lamp, standing on a small table in the passage, was burning dimly. The door to the first bedroom, in which Dan and Mary were sleeping, was slightly ajar. Silently, he moved to the half-open door of the baby's bedroom and went inside. He crept up to the cot, and with minimum disturbance to the baby, he lifted it and all the bedding out of the cot and held the whole bundle in his arms. He felt the baby stir briefly, but it did not cry. He moved silently along the passage and down the stairs, avoiding the creaking step. He left by the door, and walked to where Mason and the buggy were waiting. He laid the baby on the seat of the buggy, then spoke to Mason.

'What we do now,' he said, 'is head north, and get as far as we can from here before the baby is missed.'

They started off, Naylor driving the buggy, his horse tied on behind, and Mason riding his own horse.

When Matt Barton, in hiding in Arkansas, and not yet fully recovered from gunshot wounds received during his brush with the law, had hired Naylor, his instructions had been clear. Naylor, a cowhand turned criminal, was to remove the baby from the Diamond B, take it well away from the ranch, kill it, and make sure the body would never be found. Barton had explained that this was in revenge for the deaths of his father and brother, which had been brought about by Dan. And he had offered

Naylor a large payment for his services. Naylor had taken on Mason, with whom he had worked a few times in the past, to help him. The two men had ridden together to the Texas Panhandle. After the baby had been taken they were to part company. Mason was going to ride to Dodge City, while Naylor intended to head for Colorado.

All through the remainder of the night, with just an occasional stop, Naylor, accompanied by Mason, drove the buggy northward, with the baby lying on the seat by his side. At daybreak they had reached a point not far from the Kansas border. They stopped close to a small grove of trees, and Naylor stepped down out of the buggy, picked up the baby and bedding, and laid them on the ground. Then he removed a small spade which was tied on to the back of the buggy.

'This spot'll do,' he said to Mason. 'I know you're in a hurry to get to Dodge. You can leave now. Take the buggy, and hide it somewhere well away from here. Turn the horse loose. And here's what I owe you.'

He handed Mason a number of banknotes, then watched as his partner drove the buggy off to the east, with his horse tied behind. The baby, who had remained quiet through most of the journey, started to cry. Naylor picked him up, and carried him to the centre of the grove, then went back for

114

his horse and the spade.

He dug a hole in the ground, large enough for his purpose, then picked the baby up off the bedding. As he did so, the child stopped crying, and started kicking his legs. Naylor placed him on the bare ground, then knelt down with the bedding in his hands. He leaned forward, with the intention of suffocating the baby.

Naylor was a ruthless outlaw, who had never felt any qualms about shooting down innocent people in the course of his criminal activities. But as he bent down over baby William, a minute spark of decency in his character, hitherto dormant, kindled an overpowering feeling of revulsion against any action which would result in the death of this child. Cursing, he straightened up. The dilemma now facing him was how to keep the baby alive, and at the same time make his own escape from the consequences of the kidnapping.

Still wrestling with the problem, he carried the child out of the grove and laid him on the bedding on the ground. Then he filled in the hole he had dug, hid the spade in some undergrowth, and led his horse out of the grove. As he emerged, and glanced towards the south, he saw the distant shape of a covered wagon moving slowly in his direction. It was the type of wagon which, starting in 1841, had taken pioneers on their perilous 2,000-mile westward journey across the continent, in search of a better life for themselves and their families.

The appearance of the covered wagon could, thought Naylor, provide a solution to his problem. While waiting for its arrival, he thought up a plausible story to explain his presence there, with the baby. As the wagon, with a cow following behind, drew close, Naylor waved at the man and woman walking close by it. The wagon veered, came up to him, and stopped. He could see a young child inside it, looking out at him over the seat. The woman heard William crying, and walked up to look down at the baby lying on the ground. Startled, she looked at Naylor.

'I sure am glad to see you folks,' said Naylor. 'Let me tell you first, this baby ain't mine. The parents are both dead. How I come by it is a long story. I'll tell you later. But first, I've been carrying the child for the last five hours, and I reckon it needs some attention, including food and drink. I'm hoping you can help me with that.'

'Poor mite,' said Ellen Wilson, a slim, pleasant woman in her early thirties. She bent down to pick William up. 'You're sure right about this baby needing attention. I'll see to it right now. We've got plenty of milk. But wait till I come back before you tell how you came by this child.'

While waiting for the woman to return, Naylor chatted with her husband. Naylor gave his name as

Holt. Wilson was a big man, with a strong rugged face, a little older than his wife. Naylor asked him where they were headed.

'We're moving north till we hit the old Oregon Trail,' said Wilson. 'Then we turn west, and head for Laramie. Then we leave the Oregon Trail and head north through Wyoming. We've heard of a valley in the north of the Wyoming Territory where there's plenty of water, the ground is good for crops, and there's ample room for more settlers. That's where we aim to claim our quarter section.'

When Ellen Wilson had cleaned and fed the baby, she returned to the men.

'That's a bonny baby,' she said. 'What's his name?'

'I don't know his first name,' said Naylor, 'but his parents were called Turner.'

He went on to tell them that he had come across the baby and his parents near the border with the Indian Territory.

'They were in a covered wagon just like this,' he said. 'It was standing there, with nobody moving outside. I heard a baby crying, and when I climbed inside, I found the baby, a dead man, and a woman who was pretty far gone. But she was still able to speak. She told me that she and her husband had drunk water from a well a few miles back, and she figured it must have been poisoned. She said that none of the water had been given to the baby.

117

Then she told me that they had no kin alive, either back East or out West. She begged me to see that the baby got a good home. I couldn't do anything to help her, and a few minutes later she died.'

'That's a sad story,' said Ellen Wilson. 'I guess we've been lucky to get so far without no trouble. What happened next?'

'I buried the parents,' said Naylor, 'and turned the animals loose. Then I rode this way with the baby. I was heading for a small town about twenty miles west of here, where I could get the baby looked after, and report the deaths of the parents. But now I've met up with you, I'm wondering whether you'd take the baby with you. I can't see myself finding a better home for him than he'd get with you two in Wyoming.'

Naylor was a very convincing liar. Ellen Wilson looked at her husband. 'What d'you think, Seb?' she asked. 'When he's growed a bit, he'll be good company for Rachel.'

Her husband did not hesitate. 'Whatever you decide on this, Ellen,' he said, 'is fine by me.'

Ellen smiled at him, then spoke to Naylor.

'In that case,' she said, 'you can rest easy that you've found the baby a good home.'

'I'm real glad to hear that,' said naylor. He handed over some banknotes he said he had found in the wagon. He told them he hadn't been able to find any papers giving information about the Turners. Then, after telling them that he would report the deaths of the Turners, he parted from the Wilsons, and rode off to the west. Soon after his departure the covered wagon started moving towards the Oregon Trail.

A couple of months later, after an uneventful journey, and with baby William thriving, they drove into the valley in northern Wyoming which had been their goal. They found it to be everything they had hoped for, and filed a claim for a quarter section on the riverbank, close to other homesteaders who had arrived there the previous year.

ELEVEN

On the Diamond B, in the Texas Panhandle, the absence of the baby was not discovered until Mary woke at dawn, just as a heavy rainstorm was easing off. She went into the adjacent bedroom. Aghast, she stared at the cot, empty of both the child and the bedding. Then she screamed, and Dan ran into the room to join her. Frantic, they rushed downstairs, to find no sign of the baby there. Dan called the men from the bunkhouse. When they had assembled outside the house, he noticed that Naylor was missing.

'Where's Naylor,' he asked. Gummer told him how he had left Naylor in the saloon in Larraby the previous evening.

'The baby's gone missing,' said Dan, 'sometime after one in the morning. First we'll search in and around all the buildings for any sign of him. If nothing turns up, we'll all meet back here.'

The search having proved fruitless, Dan spoke

to the hands.

'I have a feeling,' he said, 'that Matt Barton could be behind this, and that Naylor is working for him. That rain's spoilt any chance of us picking up any tracks leading away from here. I'm riding to Larraby, to check up on Naylor.'

He told the hands to scour the surrounding area, and to be back at the ranch house by noon. He asked Jesse to take charge of the search.

The men left and, desperately worried, Dan and Mary discussed the situation. Mary was close to tears.

'You really think Matt Barton is behind this, Dan?' she asked.

'I do,' he said, 'knowing the sort of man he is. But he'd never risk coming out of hiding and doing the job himself. So I reckon he got Naylor to do his dirty work for him.'

'And what will Naylor do with William?' asked Mary.

'I just don't know,' replied Dan, although, privately, he feared that the object of the kidnapping was not to demand a ransom, but to kill the child. 'Let's see what we can find out in Larraby.'

When they arrived there they went straight to the store, where they told Mary's father about the baby's disappearance. Warren was badly shocked by the news. He went with them to see the barkeep, who told them that Naylor had not joined a poker game after Gummer had left him, but had stayed at the bar for a while before leaving himself.

'He was chatting at the bar with a stranger,' said the barkeep, 'but I don't think they knew one another. The stranger left before Naylor.'

'What was the stranger doing in town?' asked Dan.

'I don't know,' replied the barkeep. 'Maybe the liveryman could tell you.'

Dan and Warren went to see Harper, who told them that the stranger was called Mason. He had hired a buggy the previous afternoon, saying he wanted to take a look round the surrounding area, and would return the buggy in a couple of days. 'Since then,' Harper went on, 'I haven't seen him.'

'Mason and Naylor *could* have been working together,' said Dan. 'I told Jesse to bring the hands here if the search down there had turned up nothing worthwhile. Maybe we can get some help from the men in town to search for any sign of Naylor and the baby, and Mason and the buggy.'

'I can arrange that,' said Warren. When Flint and the hands turned up later with a negative report, Warren quickly mustered six townsmen. They and the ranch hands, with Dan and Mary, spent the rest of the day scouring the area. But they all returned, late in the evening, to report that the search had been completely fruitless.

'If the baby was taken soon after Mary left his bedroom,' said Dan, acutely conscious of his wife's deep distress over the continued absence of their child, 'he could be a long way from here by now. We need help. I'm riding through the night to Amarillo to see the US marshal there. I'm going to ask him to advise all law officers within three hundred miles of here to keep an eye on stagecoach passengers, and to watch out for Naylor and Mason, and the buggy and the baby. Then I'll ride back to the ranch, and we'll wait there for news.'

Half an hour later Dan left Mary with her father and rode off towards Amarillo. Arriving there the following day, he went straight to the US marshal's office. The marshal remembered him as the man responsible for bringing the Bartons to justice. Dan told him about the kidnapping, and asked him if he would help in the search for the missing baby.

'Sure,' said the marshal. 'You give me descriptions of Naylor and Mason, and I'll alert all law officers within three hundred miles of Larraby to watch out for the two men and the baby, and to check whether they've already been sighted. We'll start on this as soon as you've left, and we'll get word to you on the Diamond B of any developments.'

Dan gave the descriptions, including the fact that Naylor had sandy hair, and a missing tip to the first finger of his left hand. He thanked the marshal, and rode off towards the ranch. He arrived there in the early hours of the morning, and told Mary what had happened.

'I know it's hard, Mary,' he said, 'but we can't do

much else except wait for news, and hope for the best. I'm tuckered out. I'm going to try and get some sleep.'

They lay down together, and fell into a fitful slumber.

Two days later, with no news yet from Amarillo, a stranger rode up to the ranch house. He told Dan and Mary that his name was Anderson, and that he was a stagecoach driver.

'I've come from Larraby,' he said. 'I'm on leave right now, and I was riding south to visit some kinfolk. I called in the saloon in Larraby, and heard the news about your baby going missing. On the day that happened, I was driving a westbound stage near the southern border of Kansas, north of here. It weren't long before noon. A rider cut across ahead of me, riding north-west. He was holding a big bundle in both arms. Looked like he was carrying a baby, wrapped up. Now maybe there's a simple explanation for this, but I figured you'd like to know.'

Dan glanced at Mary. She was sitting rigid in her chair, staring at Anderson.

'We appreciate you calling by,' said Dan. 'So far we've heard of no sightings of the baby. Did you get a good look at the man?'

'He was too far off,' replied Anderson. 'All I can say is, I noticed nothing particular about him. But I *can* say that the horse he was riding was a piebald.'

Dan and Mary exchanged glances.

'It so happens,' said Dan, 'that the man we suspect of kidnapping the baby was riding a piebald. Were there any buildings in sight when you spotted him?'

Anderson shook his head. 'Not in any direction,' he replied.

'This must be followed up,' said Dan. 'My wife and I will ride north overnight to the place where you saw the man. Can you give us some landmarks to help us find the spot?'

Anderson drew a rough sketch for them on a sheet of paper. He wished them luck in their search. They thanked him, and he departed.

Dan called Jesse Flint in and told him about the sighting. He asked Flint to take charge while he and Mary went to investigate.

They rode off to the north late in the evening, and arrived at their destination at daybreak. Using the map, it was not long before they located the place where the sighting had occurred. They stopped on the trail, and looked around, confirming the driver's statement that there were no habitations in sight.

'The man was riding north-west, Mary,' said Dan. 'Let's head in the same direction, and see what turns up.'

After riding for four miles they topped a rise. Half a mile ahead of them they saw the buildings of a solitary homestead. They rode on towards it, and as they drew close to the house, a man and a woman, who had observed their approach from inside, came out and stood waiting to greet them. Dan and Mary stopped in front of them.

'Howdy folks,' said Dan. 'My name's Kincaid, and this is my wife. We're in real trouble, and there's just a chance you can help us.'

'Land's sakes,' said the woman, sensing the deep distress of the two strangers. 'Get down off those horses and come inside. Then you can tell us about it.'

In the small living room Dan told the story of the kidnapping of their child three days earlier.

'Yesterday,' he went on, 'a stagecoach driver called to see us, and said that three days ago, a little before noon, he saw a man riding across the trail in front of him, heading north-west, in this direction. The man was carrying what looked like a baby. We figured there was just a chance he might have been carrying William. Did you see anything of this man?'

'I'm real sorry that you've had a wasted journey,' said the homesteader's wife. 'The man was a friend of ours. He runs a homestead nine miles south-east of here. His wife was real sick. So sick she couldn't look after their baby. So he brought the baby here for us to mind before he went on to get the doctor to come out to the homestead. He called here for the baby yesterday afternoon.'

Seeing that Mary was close to tears, the woman comforted her. Mary and Dan stayed on for a while, and had a meal with the homesteaders. Then they set off on the long ride back to the Diamond B.

The following morning they got a message from Amarillo to say that the search had shown up nothing yet, and that it had been extended to cover a wider area.

Day after day passed without news. This stretched into weeks, until Dan and Mary, both suffering in their own way, began to resign themselves to the probability that they would never see baby William again. Then, out of the blue came a message from Sheriff Lumley at Saddle Rock in Colorado. Lumley, under whom Dan had served as a deputy sheriff, was a close friend of his. The message read: MIGHTY SORRY TO HEAR ABOUT MISSING BABY. AM HOLDING MAN CHARGED WITH BANK ROBBERY AND WAITING TRIAL. GIVES NAME AS REDFORD. NO CRIME RECORD IN COLORADO. IS AVERAGE HEIGHT, WITH SANDY HAIR AND MISSING FINGER TIP LEFT HAND. COULD BE NAYLOR. REQUEST YOU COME TO IDENTIFY AS EARLY AS POSSIBLE. SHERIFF LUMLEY SADDLE ROCK COLORADO.

Dan showed the message to Mary, saying he would catch the first stagecoach north, and would let her know by telegraph whether or not the man was Naylor. But she insisted on going with him.

They left Larraby later in the day, and arrived in Saddle Rock a little after noon the following day. They went straight to the sheriff's office. Lumley was seated at a desk inside. He rose as he saw Dan and Mary enter the office. He walked round the desk to meet them. He was a tall keen-eyed man, a little older than Dan, with a neat black moustache.

'Figured I'd see you today, Dan,' he said, as he shook hands.

Dan introduced Mary, and Lumley expressed his sympathy over the prolonged loss of their child.

'If the man I'm holding in one of the cells back there *is* Naylor,' he said, 'then maybe you can find out exactly what's happened to the baby. I take it you're pretty sure he was the one who took the baby from the house?'

'Pretty sure,' said Dan. 'He'd been with us less than two weeks, and he'd helped carry furniture up to the baby's bedroom. So he knew exactly where it was located. And I have a strong hunch now that a letter of recommendation from a trail boss that he showed me was a fake.'

'Right,' said the sheriff. 'But before I take you to see the prisoner, let me tell you how he landed in jail. He tried to rob the bank in town, single handed. But he didn't make it. By pure chance I was with the manager in his office while the robber was holding a gun on the teller. A while back, the manager had got a telegraph key fitted under the counter where the teller stood, so that he could press on it with his foot, and operate a sounder in the manager's office in case of trouble.

'We heard the alarm sound, and the manager saw what was happening through a small hole cut in the wall which gives him a view of the counter. To try and avoid any bloodshed, I slipped out of the building through a rear door, and I was waiting just outside the front door when the robber came out carrying the loot. I pistol-whipped him over the head and put him in jail. He's not wanted for any other crimes that we know of, so I reckon that unless anything else turns up, the judge'll sentence him to a spell in the state penitentiary. Can't say how long. I'm expecting the judge in four or five days. Now let's go and see the prisoner.'

Lumley led them through a door into a space containing three cells. Only one was in use. The single occupant was lying on a bunk. Dan recognized him immediately.

'That's Naylor,' he told the sheriff. Then he and Mary stood looking through the bars at the man they believed had so cruelly deprived them of their child. It was a moment before Naylor realized the identity of the couple standing by the sheriff. Then his eyes widened. He rose quickly to his feet and stood staring at Dan and Mary. The sheriff opened the cell door and walked inside, followed by the others. Naylor retreated, and stood with his back against the wall.

'I reckon you know these folks, Naylor,' said Lumley. 'They've been telling me some mighty interesting things about you. As well as being a robber, it seems you're a baby kidnapper.'

Shocked at the sight of Dan and Mary, Naylor avoided meeting their eyes. He spoke to the sheriff. There was a note of panic in his voice.

'You ain't got no proof of that,' he said.

'Only the facts,' said Dan, 'that after turning up as a stranger at the Diamond B, you worked less than two weeks before disappearing at the same time as our baby; you knew where the baby's bed was located, and you were seen talking to a stranger who'd hired a buggy that was never returned. Where is our baby, Naylor? What did you do with the child?'

Naylor, rueing the day that he had succumbed to the temptation of a high reward for carrying out the assignment given him by Barton, stayed silent.

'The way things look to me,' said the sheriff, 'on account of the baby still being missing after all this time, and you being the one who took him, I reckon you can be brought to trial for murder. I can't speak for the jury, but the odds are that you're heading for the hangman's noose. So if the child ain't dead, now's the time to tell us just what

130

happened. Think about it. We'll leave you now, but sing out as soon as you feel like talking.'

They left Naylor and went to sit in the office. It took the prisoner only ten minutes to reach a decision and he called out. The sheriff, with Dan and Mary, went back into Naylor's cell.

The prisoner gave a full and true account of the episode, with the exception that he said that there had never been any intention of killing the baby. Barton's instructions had been that the child be left some place where his parents would never find him.

'Those folks who took the baby,' said Dan. 'What was their name?'

'I don't recollect they told me,' said Naylor, 'and that's the truth.'

'And you told us the valley they were heading for is in north Wyoming,' said Dan. 'They gave you no idea just where? That's a big area, with plenty of places where a homesteader might settle.'

'No, they didn't,' Naylor replied.

'Do you know where Barton is now?' asked the sheriff.

'I don't,' replied Naylor. 'I met him by arrangement on the border between the Indian Territory and Arkansas, but I don't know where he came from or where he was going when we parted.'

Mary and Dan asked Naylor a few more questions about the covered wagon and the family who had taken baby William into their care. During this conversation the prisoner told them that he recollected that the first name of the woman was Ellen, and that their child was called Rachel. They returned to the office with Lumley.

'My guess is,' said the sheriff, 'that Naylor's telling the truth about what happened to the baby, and he's hoping, for his own sake, that you'll find the child.'

'I reckon you're right,' said Dan, looking at Mary. He could see that her dwindling hope of ever finding their baby again had been rekindled by this turn of events. He felt the same way himself.

'We'll go by stage to north Wyoming,' he said. 'Then we'll get a couple of horses and start the search. A covered wagon moves pretty slow, but I reckon that the one Naylor told us about should have reached north Wyoming by now. We know that they aim to settle in a valley. That should narrow down the search a bit.'

'There's a northbound stage leaving three hours from now,' said Lumley. 'I'll ask the judge to postpone the trial. You let us know whether or not you've been able to find the baby. And I sure hope the news we get from you is good.'

Dan and Mary left on the stage three hours later. When they arrived in Cheyenne, in the south of Wyoming Territory, they found an office where the claims for homesteads were recorded. Here they were able to find out the areas where homesteaders had already settled in valleys in the northern half of the territory. The names of the homesteaders were also recorded, but this fact was of no use to Dan and Mary because they did not know the surname of the people they were looking for. In any case, thought Dan, their claim might not yet be recorded.

They got a copy of the map on which the valleys were shown, then went to the hotel where they planned to stay the night. Their intention was to take a northbound stage in the morning. They looked at the map together, and decided that the best place to leave the stage would be a town called Stony River, well within the northern section of Wyoming Territory, and not far from the border with South Dakota.

'We'll buy a couple of horses,' said Dan, 'and start our search from there, working our way west. It may take a while, Mary, but I have a strong feeling that in the end you'll be holding baby William in your arms once again.'

TWELVE

Dan and Mary arrived in Stony River a little before noon. They went to the livery stable to get two horses. The liveryman told them that no covered wagons had passed through town for the past two months. They went on to the general store, where they bought provisions and bedrolls for camping out. Then, following the map, they embarked on a systematic search for their baby.

The procedure they adopted was to ride into a valley and call at the first homestead they came to. They knew that a group of homesteaders in a particular area generally formed a closely knit community. They asked at the homestead whether they knew of any settlers with a baby boy and a small girl who had arrived recently in the valley. The mother's first name was Ellen, and the girl was called Rachel.

The first ten days of their search produced no result, and at their overnight camps, Dan could see

134

that Mary was growing despondent. He tried to reassure her.

'We ain't finished yet, Mary,' he said. 'There are more places to visit. Let's hope our luck changes soon.'

The following morning they rode into a valley and headed for a homestead stretching back from the bank of the river. They could see a man working in one of the fields.

Six miles further up the valley, past the last of the homesteads lined up along the river bank, the covered wagon belonging to Seb and Ellen Wilson was standing, on the quarter section on which Seb had filed a claim. They had selected a position for the house, and were now awaiting delivery of materials required for its construction. For the time being they were using the wagon as their home.

Dan and Mary rode up to the man working in the field. He saw them approaching, and straightened up to greet them. His name was Lawton.

'Howdy,' said Dan. 'Maybe you can help us. We're looking for a family from back East who came to north Wyoming in a covered wagon during the last few weeks. They were looking for a quarter section to settle on. They had a baby boy and a little girl with them. Have you seen anything of them here in the valley?'

'Only one wagon showed up during the last three months,' said Lawton, 'and that was about two weeks ago. I saw the wagon passing by. It had a black cover, which struck me as unusual on a covered wagon of this sort. I ain't met the folks who were with it yet, but I heard from one of my neighbours who called in a few days ago that they have one child, a little girl. Seems they've put in a claim for a quarter section about six miles up the valley. We're figuring to go visit them tomorrow to offer some help with building the house when they need it.'

They thanked Lawton and rode off in the direction from which they had come, intending to leave the valley and head for the next area on the list of those to be checked.

'I thought for a minute there, Mary,' said Dan, 'that maybe we'd reached the end of our search. But the single child and the black cover rule the new arrivals out. Naylor was quite clear about the wagon having a *white* cover. Let's ride on as far as we can before dark.'

Lawton stood watching the two riders as they headed down the valley. Then, as he turned to resume his work, he saw his wife driving their buckboard down the valley towards him. She waved to him as she passed, drove up to the house and went inside. She had been visiting a friend, the wife of the homesteader on the adjacent quarter section.

Lawton worked on for a short while, then went into the house. Chatting about her visit, his wife mentioned that her friend had told her that the new arrivals had, contrary to what they had been told earlier, *two* children, one little girl of their own, and one baby boy who had been adopted. Lawton told her of the recent visit by Dan and Mary.

'I think I should let them know about the baby boy,' he said. 'I have a feeling it's something they'd really want to know about. I'll chase after them. They ain't been gone that long.'

He left the house, quickly saddled his horse, and raced off after Dan and Mary. He caught up with them just as they were about to ride out of the valley after taking a short rest. Surprised to see him, they listened with mounting excitement as he told them about the adopted baby boy.

'We're mighty obliged to you for letting us know this,' said Dan, and went on to tell Lawton of the kidnapping of their baby and their belief that he could be somewhere in north Wyoming.

'I guess you'll be riding back with me, then,' said Lawton, 'and then on to see the Wilsons. According to my wife, that's their name.'

'You're dead right,' said Dan. 'We can't wait to see the baby.'

They left Lawton at his homestead, and rode quickly on, with a mixture of happy anticipation that they were about to recover heir baby, and fear that they were going to be disappointed.

At last, in the distance, they caught sight of the wagon, with its distinctive black cover. As they drew near they saw a man and a woman standing near the wagon, with a little girl playing close by. Curious, the couple watched Dan and Mary as they approached and stopped in front of them. At the same time, the sound of a baby crying came from inside the wagon, but lasted only briefly. Mary's hopes rose. The sound she had just heard seemed familiar.

'I guess you're the Wilsons,' said Dan. 'I'm Dan Kincaid, and this is my wife Mary. I'll come right to the point. We think that you might have a baby boy in the wagon there who was kidnapped from our ranch in the Texas Panhandle, and handed over to you by a man you met near the Kansas border. This man is now in jail.' Dan went on to repeat Naylor's account of the handing over of the baby, and the story he told the Wilsons about the death of the child's parents.

Astonished, the Wilsons listened to Dan's account, then the homesteader spoke.

'It all happened just like you told it,' he said. 'He sure fooled us.'

Dan showed Wilson a letter from Sheriff Lumley

confirming his story, and Mary told Ellen Wilson of the purple birthmark on the middle of baby William's back.

'That's enough for me,' said Ellen. 'I can imagine what you've been through. Come with me.'

Mary quickly dismounted and ran after Ellen to the wagon. A moment later she ran back to Dan, half-laughing, half-crying, with the baby cradled in her arms.

'He's a bonny baby,' said Ellen Wilson, 'and I'm sure going to miss him. But six months or so from now I'll be having another baby of my own to look after.'

They talked for a while, and it turned out that the white wagon cover had been badly damaged by a twister near Cheyenne, and that the only material they could get to replace it was black. Wilson offered to take Mary and the baby on the buckboard, with Dan riding alongside, to the nearest point where they could sell their horses and catch a stagecoach.

They left soon after, and when they reached Cheyenne Dan sent a telegraph message to Sheriff Lumley, informing him that the baby had been found, safe and well. Then they continued on their journey, happy and relieved that after the weeks of worry and despair, their family was once again complete.

There was great rejoicing on the Diamond B when they returned. Dan told the hands, after Mary had taken the baby into the ranch house, how Naylor had helped them towards a successful outcome of their search.

'Now you all know,' he went on, 'that Matt Barton was behind the kidnapping. He's dead set on taking revenge on me because I was responsible for his father and brother being captured and hanged. This may not be the end of the matter. He may still come after me or Mary or the baby, or get somebody else to do his dirty work. Mary and I will make sure the baby's guarded at all times, but I'm asking you men to be on the watch for any strangers around here, or anything unusual happening.'

'You can count on us,' said Flint, and the men dispersed.

A few days later Dan got a message from Sheriff Lumley telling him that Naylor had been tried for robbery and kidnapping, and had received a long custodial sentence.

Inside the house Dan strengthened the window- and door-fastenings, so that they could not be forced without a considerable amount of noise. Baby William's cot was moved into the bedroom of his parents. Then, remembering Sheriff Lumley's account of the alarm system in the bank in Saddle Rock, Dan rode into Larraby to see the telegraph operator. He asked him whether the telegraph maintenance engineer was likely to be in town in the near future.

'He's due here tomorrow,' said the operator. 'He's coming to fit some new batteries.'

Dan rode into town the following day to enlist the help of the engineer in improving the security at the ranch. He waited until the man had completed the battery replacement, then discussed the matter with him, mentioning the alarm system in the bank at Saddle Rock.

'What I have in mind,' said Dan, 'is something I could lay on the ground outside the door and the three windows of the ranch house that would warn us during the night of any prowlers outside, by sending a signal to a sounder in the bedroom, and to another one in the bunkhouse.'

'It can be done,' said the engineer, 'with the help of the blacksmith. I'll get permission from headquarters to help you with this, then we'll go to see him.'

Ten minutes later they went to find the blacksmith, who agreed to help. An assembly was constructed, composed of two pieces of flexible metal sheeting, fixed one above the other in a wooden framework. The sheets were well insulated from one another, and only came into contact when the upper sheet was stepped on. A wire connection could be made to each sheet.

The engineer expressed his satisfaction with the first assembly, and the blacksmith promised to finish the remaining three during the day. It was arranged that the engineer should bring the four assemblies to the Diamond B the following morning, when he would install the alarm system.

Next day the engineer arrived early at the ranch, where he laid the four sets of alarm plates in position, and connected them by insulated wires to a battery and to sounders in the bedroom of Dan and Mary and in the bunkhouse. He adjusted the sounders to give the loudest possible noise.

The system was tried out and proved to be highly effective. After the engineer had departed, Dan discussed security with the hands, and made sure there were enough weapons held in the bunkhouse for the men to use against any intruders attempting to get into the ranch house.

THIRTEEN

After being wounded in his clash with the law in the Indian Territory, Matt Barton had gone into hiding at a small farm in Arkansas owned by a relative of his, and not far from the Texas border. When a contact of his in the Texas Panhandle sent him news of the kidnapping of baby William, he received this with great satisfaction. His twisted mind gloated over the intense distress the permanent disappearance of the baby must have caused Dan and Mary.

So when the news came some time later, from the same source, that the baby was still alive, and had been returned to his parents, Barton was enraged at Naylor's failure to complete the work for which he had been paid. Then, a little later, the news came that Naylor was serving time in prison. Barton's wounds were now healed, and he was determined to pursue his insane desire for vengeance. He had plenty of funds from the proceeds of past robberies to enable him to hire some help of the right calibre.

He rode into the Indian Territory, to a haven for criminals, known to himself, but not, as yet, to the law. There, by offering rich rewards for their services, he recruited two past acquaintances, both on the run from crimes committed in Kansas. The two men, Jefferson and Price, were both hardened criminals, wanted for both murder and robbery. They had often worked together in the past. Both men were of medium height, still in their thirties. Jefferson was slim, with a cruel narrow face, while Price was stocky, with a round, open face which belied his ruthless character.

Barton had explained that his main objective was the death of Dan, but said that the rancher's wife could be killed if she got in the way.

'We'll ride to the Texas Panhandle,' said Barton. 'I know a place where we can hide out north-east of the Diamond B. It's a cave in the side of a ravine, well off the beaten track. We'll hole up there to plan the operation.'

Near the end of a long ride they picked up a good supply of provisions at a small settlement and rode on to their destination. The cave, in a secluded ravine, was big enough to accommodate all three in comfort. It was dry inside, and there were no indications that it had been occupied recently. After they had taken a meal Barton spoke to Price.

'There's a homestead between here and the Diamond B,' he said. 'Ride there in the morning. Pretend you're just passing through. Without raising it yourself, see if you can get the folks there talking about the kidnapping of the baby, and whether the Kincaids and the baby are all at the ranch right now. Then come back here.'

Just under an hour later Price rode up to the homestead. He stopped outside the house just as the door opened and the homesteader, Vickery, came out, closely followed by his wife.

'Howdy,' said Price, smiling down on them. 'If you can spare it, I'd be obliged if my horse could take a drink.'

'Help yourself,' said Vickery, pointing to a nearby water trough, 'and when you're finished, there's a pot of coffee on the stove, if you'd like to sample it.'

'Sounds good to me,' said Price. When he had watered his horse he followed Vickery, a naturally loquacious man, into the house, where he told them that he was on his way to visit kinfolk in New Mexico Territory.

'That's mighty good coffee,' said Price, then went on to comment on the isolated position of the homestead.

'I guess you don't see many visitors,' he said,

'and things stay pretty quiet around here?'

Vickery's eyebrows lifted. 'You ain't heard about the baby being kidnapped, then?' he asked. 'There was a real hullabaloo when that happened.'

Price professed ignorance of the event, and Vickery went on to tell him at length of the episode.

'Well, I'm darned,' said Price. 'Seems to me that's about as low as anybody can get, kidnapping a baby boy like that. The parents must have gone through hell. Have they carried on ranching?'

'Yes,' replied Vickery. 'They're on the Diamond B with the baby. I heard that Kincaid aims to build up his herd.'

If the homesteader had known of the alarm system set up at the ranch, he would no doubt have told Price about that, too. But Dan had made sure that it was a closely guarded secret, known only to the blacksmith, the telegraph engineer and operator, and those at the ranch.

After chatting with the homesteaders for a while on other matters, Price departed, riding off in a westerly direction till he was out of sight of the homestead. Then he swung round and headed for the hideout.

When he arrived at the cave Barton listened with interest to his account of the conversation with the homesteaders.

'That's good news,' he said. 'We can go ahead

with our operation. When I was laid up in Arkansas, I figured the best way of paying Kincaid back for getting my father and brother hanged was to take his baby from him. But now that I'm fit enough to go after him myself, I want to kill him, and I want him to know that it's me who's doing it.

'We'll leave here for the ranch at midnight. I guess the buildings are much the same as they were when I was living there. First, we'll check whether there are any guards posted outside the buildings. If not, it shouldn't be too hard to force our way into the house, without waking anybody. There's only one double bedroom, and that's right at the top of the stairs. That's where Kincaid and his wife will be. Jefferson and I will go in there with a lighted lamp, while Price stands guard outside the house. Then I'll wake Kincaid, and shoot him dead. When that's done, we'll leave, and head for the Indian Territory.'

This plan was agreed, and they stayed at the cave until midnight. When they reached the vicinity of the ranch buildings they halted. They could see no lights. Barton sent Jefferson on to circle the buildings at a safe distance to check whether any guards had been posted. He returned twenty minutes later to report that he could see no sign of guards, and it was safe for them to approach the ranch house. They picketed their horses and walked towards the house. They stopped near the door.

'Wait here,' said Barton to the others. Then he approached the door and checked it. It was stoutly built and securely fastened. He moved to a side window, examined it as best he could in the darkness, then went on to check the remaining windows. He returned to the others. He spoke quietly.

'The best place to break in,' he said, 'is through the window at the back. It's not as strong as the others, and it's the one furthest from the bedroom.'

He told Price to stay where he was, on guard. Then he and Jefferson walked round to the rear of the house.

In the bedroom Dan woke instantly as Barton stepped on the alarm device outside the door of the house, and the sounder, on a bedside table, close to his head, gave a loud chatter. He woke Mary, and they dressed hurriedly.

'Like we agreed, Mary,' said Dan, handing her a loaded shotgun, 'you stay in here with the baby. I'll go downstairs and fight them off with the help of the hands as they try to break in. If I, or any of the hands come up to this room, we'll call out to you as we climb the stairs. If anybody else comes up, use the shotgun.'

As they were dressing, and Dan was speaking, they heard the chatter of the sounder repeated

148

three times as Barton moved around the house.

In the bunkhouse Flint was the first to hear the sounder. He roused the other three hands. Quickly, they all dressed and picked up their six-guns, already loaded, without lighting a lamp inside the bunkhouse. Then they left the building by a rear door, not visible from the ranch house, and screened by the cookshack, to which they ran up and waited.

Inside the ranch house, when Dan left Mary and the baby he went downstairs and listened at the door and the windows. At the rear window, he could hear the faint sound of somebody outside attempting to force it without making a lot of noise. He thought he could hear two muted voices. Knowing that to force an entry quietly would take some time he moved quickly to a trapdoor in the floor against a side wall of the house, lifted it, and dropped into a trench, the top of which was boarded over. The trench led to the side of the cookshack, where the hands were standing. Dan pushed a trapdoor up and climbed out to join them.

'There's somebody trying to get in through the window in the back wall,' he said. 'It sounded like two men. It could be Barton, with somebody helping him. And maybe he's got more than one man with him. We'd best get moving. You all know what to do. And remember, the odds are that the men outside the ranch house are all killers and handy with their weapons. So take care.'

Harley, the cook, stayed where he was. The others moved through the darkness to previously selected points around the house, just outside the range of vision of the intruders. Each of these points provided cover from gunfire. Dan was behind the privy, facing the rear of the ranch house. The other three were behind a buckboard, a large water trough, and a small storage shed.

Dan was the first to open fire, aiming a few shots in the direction of the rear window of the ranch house. The hands immediately followed suit, so that shots were directed towards the other three sides of the building, making it clear that the ranch house was surrounded.

Barton and the others were taken entirely by surprise. Their one thought was to reach their horses and make a quick getaway. Jefferson and Barton moved away from the window at the rear of the house, firing in Dan's direction as they did so. Dan returned the fire with six rapid shots from a second six-gun which he had tucked under his belt. Jefferson went down and stayed there. Barton staggered as a bullet struck him in the side. Then, limping badly, he moved round to the side of the house which Flint, behind the buckboard, was facing.

The quickest route between the house and the

picketed horses passed close by the buckboard, and Flint saw Price, as yet unhit, running towards him. He fired the last two shots in his six-gun at the approaching figure, and Price went down. A moment later Flint saw Barton limping towards him, and reached for the second six-gun tucked under his belt. But before he could draw it out and fire, a bullet from Barton's gun grazed the side of his head, and he collapsed on the ground. Barton disappeared into the darkness.

When Dan and the other hands found Flint a little later, after discovering the bodies of Price and Jefferson, he was climbing unsteadily to his feet. He told them about the limping man who had shot him and escaped.

'The other two are both dead,' said Dan, 'and neither of them is Barton. I reckon it's likely Barton was the third man, and he was hit during the gunfire.'

He told Flint to accompany him to the ranch house, where Mary would tend to his wound, and ordered the other hands to take the two dead men into the barn, then look for their horses. Inside the house he called to tell Mary that the danger was over. She came downstairs to tend to Flint, who had a shallow graze on the temple, which was bleeding.

Shortly after, the hands returned to tell Dan they had found two horses picketed not far from the ranch house.

'The one who got away,' said Dan, 'could be a long way from here by daybreak. But we don't know how badly he's wounded. As soon as it's light enough we'll ride out and see if we can pick up any sign of him.'

After Barton shot Flint down he moved as quickly as he could to his horse, mounted it, and rode off fast in a north-easterly direction. After riding several miles he stopped to examine his wound. The flesh on his left side, just above the hip, had been badly damaged by a bullet. His shirt and pants were soaked with blood. He knew that if the flow was not stopped he would soon be incapable of riding on. He remembered that ahead of him was the Vickery homestead, recently visited by Price. He decided to get help there. Holding his padded bandanna against his side in an effort to reduce the flow of blood, he rode on.

It was still dark when he reached the homestead. He dismounted outside the house. No lights were showing inside. He led his horse into the barn and secured it. He left, closing the door behind him, and limped up to the house. He tried to open the door, but it was secured on the inside. He hammered on it with his fist. Twice he repeated this, then saw that a lamp had been lit inside the house. The door was partly opened and Vickery, holding a lamp, peered out. His wife stood behind him. Not recognizing the man outside, Vickery asked him what he wanted.

'A little way back there,' said Barton, 'I done a darn fool thing. Fell off my horse and damaged my side. It's bleeding bad. Was hoping maybe you could help me stop the bleeding. Then I'll ride on to Larraby and see the doctor.'

Briefly, Vickery hesitated. Then, seeing the blood-soaked clothing, he opened the door wide, and invited the stranger inside. Barton entered, secured the door behind him, then drew his six-gun. He ordered the Vickerys to stand in a corner of the room, and they watched him apprehensively while he searched it for weapons. He repeated the search in the rest of the house. His only find was an ancient shotgun, loaded with two cartridges which he removed and put in his pocket. He ordered his prisoners to get dressed, one at a time. Then, still holding his six-gun, he dropped the shotgun on the floor beside him and sat down sideways on a kitchen chair. He pulled up his shirt and vest, and told Emma Vickery to tend his wound. Immediately the homesteader and his wife suspected that they were looking at a gunshot wound.

'Just do as you're told,' said Barton, 'and nobody's going to get hurt. I want this wound cleaned up and disinfected, and the bleeding

153

stopped. Then you can slap a thick pad over it and bandage it up tight.'

'We're a bit short of bandaging,' said Emma Vickery with a slight tremor in her voice, 'but I'll do the best I can. As for disinfectant, we're clean out of that. We were aiming to get some more from the store today.'

Barton cursed. He was well aware of the threat of infection in a gunshot wound. He spoke to Vickery.

'You'll ride into Larraby,' he said. 'Be there when the store opens. And bring back some disinfectant and plenty of bandaging. You'll probably find out when you're in town that I'm on the run. I reckon you know better than to tell anybody I'm here. Do that, and I'll shoot you both dead. And right now I want you to go to the barn. You'll find my horse there. Wash the blood off, and hide the saddle. Then put the horse with yours.'

Emma Vickery proceeded to clean the wound, then apply a thick pad, held firmly in place by a temporary bandage. As she finished, Vickery told Barton that he would now depart for Larraby.

'Go ahead,' said Barton, 'and remember what I told you.'

He rose and walked to the window. It was just after daybreak. He watched the homesteader as he went for his horse, then rode off in the direction of Larraby. Suddenly he stiffened, then picked up the shotgun as he saw two riders approaching Vickery.

The homesteader recognized the two riders as Gummer and Ewing, both of them hands on the Diamond B. When they reached him they told him about the raid on the Diamond B and the escape, probably wounded, of one of the men involved.

'It's likely he'll be well away from here by now,' said Gummer, 'but we're checking around to see whether anybody's seen or heard him.'

'Well, he sure ain't been here,' said the homesteader. 'Like you said, he'd be in a hurry to get as far away from here as he could before daybreak. I'm heading for Larraby to pick up a few things we need from the store.'

Gummer and Ewing left Vickery and rode off in a southerly direction. Inside the house, Barton relaxed, watching them until they passed out of sight.

When the homesteader reached town he went straight to the store. He asked Warren for a large roll of bandaging and a bottle of disinfectant.

'Emma cut herself with a kitchen knife,' he explained, 'and we've run out of disinfectant and bandaging. I figure it's wise in future to keep a good supply on the homestead in case of emergencies.'

Warren asked Vickery whether he had heard about the trouble at the Diamond B, and the homesteader told him he had already received the news from Gummer and Ewing. Then he left for the homestead. When he reached it, Barton searched him for weapons. Then Emma Vickery uncovered the wound, which had stopped bleeding, treated it with disinfectant, and padded and rebandaged it. For the rest of the day the outlaw rested in an armchair by the window between meals. At no time did he allow both Vickery and his wife out of his sight at the same time. He knew that he must allow his wound some time for healing before riding on. He also knew that he needed to get some sleep.

After supper he got up from his chair and took a look at a storeroom next to the kitchen. It had a very small window, about nine inches square, in the outside wall. The door opened into the living room, and a bolt had been provided to hold it closed. After looking inside the storeroom, Barton spoke to the Vickerys.

'I aim to get some sleep,' he said, 'so I'm putting you two in the storeroom for the night, with the door bolted. I'll be sitting in an armchair facing the door: I'm a light sleeper, and if I hear you trying to force it, I'll send a load of buckshot into it from the shotgun.

In Larraby, four hours after Vickery had left the store, Doc Bellamy called in to make a few purchases. Warren mentioned the homesteader's visit for medical supplies and his account of the meeting with the two Diamond B hands. Suddenly, Bellamy's mind was working overtime.

'What you've just told me don't ring true,' he said. 'I never met a man who fussed as much as he does about the health of his wife. For advice on the slightest ailment she's suffering from, he either brings her to see me or gets me to ride out to the homestead. And I'm certain he would never willingly leave Emma alone at the homestead with the slightest chance of a wounded killer being in the area on the loose.'

'I can see what you're thinking,' said Warren. 'Dan's got to be told about this. And soon.'

'I'll ride to the ranch now, to let him know,' said Bellamy. 'I've paid quite a few visits to the homestead. Maybe I can give Dan some information about it that would be useful.'

When Bellamy reached the Diamond B Dan told him that the search of the surrounding area for the man who had escaped had been fruitless. The doctor then told him about the unusual behaviour of Vickery.

'It sure sounds like the man we're after could be hiding on the homestead,' said Dan. 'After dark I'll ride there with Flint and see if we can capture him without any harm coming to Vickery and his wife.'

The doctor gave Dan and Flint details of the homestead, particularly the layout of the interior of the house. Then he returned to Larraby.

Shortly after he had left, Dan and Flint rode off towards the homestead, leaving two hands in the living room of the house to guard Mary and the baby. It was late in the evening when they reached their destination. They picketed their horses well away from the house and approached it cautiously on foot. Light was showing through the curtains covering the living room windows.

Silently, they circled the house. Behind one of the living room windows there was a gap between the curtains, which had been unnoticed by Barton, which gave a restricted view into the room. It was just wide enough to allow Dan to see the outlaw sitting on an armchair near the door, with a shotgun lying cross his thighs. The outlaw's chin was resting on his chest and he appeared to be dozing. Dan moved aside to let Flint look in. Then they retreated from the window.

'Likely Barton's fastened the Vickerys in one of the other rooms,' said Dan. 'You keep an eye on Barton through the window, while I see if I can locate them. Let me know if he moves from the chair.'

He walked round to the rear of the house. The first window he came to was a small one which, from Bellamy's description, must lead into the storeroom. He tapped three times, very lightly, on the window pane, paused, then repeated the three taps. The window opened, and during a brief whispered conversation with Vickery Dan learnt that the homesteader and his wife were fastened in the storeroom.

'Lie down on the floor,' said Dan, 'while we take care of Barton. Don't get up till I tell you it's safe.'

Dan rejoined Flint and they decided on their next move. Flint went to the front of the house, to a position opposite a window close to the door. Dan went to the window through which Barton was visible. The outlaw was still dozing. As prearranged, Flint threw a large stone through the window close to the outlaw. The glass shattered and the stone fell on the floor inside the room, in front of Barton. Flint ran away from the window, along the front wall of the house.

Dan saw the outlaw's immediate response to the shattering of the window. Barton rose, twisted round, and fired one barrel of the shotgun through the window. As he did this, Dan broke a pane of glass with the barrel of his six-gun, pulled the curtain aside with his left hand and, just as Barton was bringing the shotgun round to bear on him, shot the outlaw through the head. Death was instantaneous. Barton collapsed, and the shotgun, with its second lethal load of buckshot still undischarged, fell to the floor beside him. Dan entered the house through the shattered front window and let Flint in. Then they let a much relieved Vickery and his wife out of the storeroom.

And so ended Matt Barton's insane quest for vengeance. With the threat finally removed, Dan and Mary concentrated on raising a family of two boys and a girl, and on building up a prosperous cattle ranch.

Home Library Service (For Staff Use Only)

1	2	3	4	5	6	7	8	9
		3 26/8						

27094